A Different Road Traveled

Rebecca Gertner

www.ADifferentRoadTraveled.com

The Strength To Stand Series
www.TheStrengthToStand.com

Creative Team Publishing
San Diego

Disclaimer:

The story and all characters depicted in this book are fiction. All facts depicted in the book are a creation of fiction or taken from public record and national headlines. Any resemblance to any known or real person, fact, circumstance, event, or situation is purely coincidental.

Resources:

- Study Questions can be found on page 287. The study questions were created to facilitate those who wish to use this book for group discussion or self-reflection.
- Information concerning safety in a stalking or abusive situation can be found on page 299. If you, or a loved one, are in a stalking or abusive situation, please contact local women's advocacy groups or domestic relationship centers as well as your local police department.
- Products and Services can be found on page 307.

ISBN: 978-0-9897975-2-8
PUBLISHED BY CREATIVE TEAM PUBLISHING
www.CreativeTeamPublishing.com
San Diego
Printed in the United States of America

Dedication

For Luke, may your legacy burn brightly in my life and the lives of our children.

My hope & strength are found in Christ alone!

1 Peter 4:11

Proverbs 31:25

Endorsements on Behalf of
A Different Road Traveled

"Rebecca Gertner tells a riveting and timely story for our day. Through her full characters' rapidly unfolding thoughts and movements, the reader is witness to the contrasting outcomes of cowardice and courage, of self-absorption and true life. A recommended novel for wide reading, and small group discussion — youth, adults, pastors, seminarians!"

~ Deanna Harrington Christiansen

Author, *Notes on a Flight Home – Selected Poetry;*

M.A., Theological Studies, Bethel Seminary San Diego, CA;

Certificate in Christian Spiritual Formation and Direction Studies, Christian Formation & Direction Ministries (CDFM), San Diego, CA;

Member, Christians for Biblical Equality, www.cbeinternational.org

"*A Different Road Traveled* reveals the importance of possessing a personal foundation, focus, and faith when life's journey deals unexpected and unpleasant circumstances. Embrace the story of young Rachel Riley's journey and find yourself identifying with her life's challenges.

"She demonstrates the importance of remaining committed to your values even when those values cause conflict with others. Her strong faith leads Rachel successfully down life's pathway revealing that anyone can choose to take a different and better road, a road of courage and faith."

~ Dennis Fredricks
Executive Director,
Sacramento Region Baptist Network

*****

"Find yourself plunged into the depths of mystery and suspense. Feel your inner voice constantly asking, 'What happens next?'

"Rebecca Gertner writes with a freshness and inspiration of faith that only comes through the crucible of life's personal demands, dangers, and difficulties.

"If you find yourself in a seemingly hopeless crisis, in this book you will find that hardships in life are like the nails that hold us to the cross, so that only in and through crucifixion can we experience resurrection power and life.

"This is the secret to living above the norm and living a dramatically different life."

~ David L. Ford

President, Globe For Christ International, Inc.

www.globeforchrist.com

.

Spring 1994

Over and over the voices hurled disturbing accusations at her. Rachel Riley sat in front of a crowd of people and she was trying desperately not to cry. With each angry insult, the tears rose higher in her throat and threatened to spill out. Forcing back her emotions, Rachel looked at the six people who held so much power. How could she make them understand? Disturbing memories played in her mind like a movie and the voices were the soundtrack. Hurt and anger, guilt and a myriad of other emotions were mixed with those memories of fear and danger, the sound of a loud truck, and a small black dog.

Rachel sat next to the judge and looked out at all the people. Among several familiar faces, she could see her parents. As she was looking at them, they stood up and started to yell at her.

"You're too conceited," they said, "You think all the boys like you."

Louder and louder the voices grew until she couldn't distinguish one from the other. Her heart was pounding in her chest and she could barely breathe. She had to say something. She had to stop the angry voices. Gathering all the courage she could find, she stood and held up her hands until one by one the people quieted. Finally, she had their attention. But she waited still, waiting until there was no sound except for the heaving of her chest as she tried to draw in a full breath. She hoped a deep breath would calm her enough to speak without her voice breaking. With every eye focused on her, she closed her eyes and opened her mouth. "It's my fault. I prayed for this."

The words were not what she wanted to say! How she wished she could snatch them back! Everyone gasped, and the chaos returned as people were once again shouting. Declarations of blame and hatred were accompanied by fists swinging in the air and fingers pointing. *Bang, bang, bang* went the gavel.

"Order, Order!" yelled the judge. But it was too late, she could see it in their eyes; the jury believed her. It was over. Rachel hung her head and sobbed.

Suddenly Rachel was no longer sitting in a witness stand. Instead, she was lying in bed. Drenched from head to toe in sweat and tears, she was cold and shivering. Thank goodness it was only a dream… this time.

Chapter 1

October 1992

She was once called a walking dictionary, which should have been a compliment, but Rachel Riley wasn't so sure the comment was made for that reason. Whether the name was meant as an insult or not, it fit and Rachel knew it.

She liked to read and was always learning new words. But every now and then she would get stumped by a word and in those instances Rachel would drag out the dictionary. Other times she would know a word but would look it up just to see why a person would have chosen to use that particular word.

And there she sat, dictionary in hand. It had been about three years since she had read the definition she was now looking at. She used to hate the word and all the ill feelings it gave her, but not anymore. Wanting to hear the definition in her own voice, she read it out loud; just like she did last time.

"Different: Unlike in form, quality, amount, or nature; distinct or separate; differing from all others; unusual: a different point of view."

Rachel's father was the pastor at Casper Community Church in the small coastal town of Casper, California. Not only was she a pastor's kid, she was homeschooled and that made her someone who was, by every definition—different.

While she was in her teens, Rachel really struggled with feeling out of place and it didn't help matters that she had a tendency to be what her parents called dramatic. But that was years ago and since then she had grown up. She was now someone who was boldly standing for what they believed in and she didn't care about fitting in anymore.

She had blossomed into a strong young woman who knew what God wanted for her and she was determined to keep focused. And these days, keeping focused was fairly easy because Rachel hardly had a moment to spare. Being the Youth Director at her father's church, as well as traveling to speak at conferences with her father and mother, she rarely thought about anything other than youth events or the topic of her next lecture. Though Dan Riley was a well-known author and speaker who spoke several times a year, Rachel, too, was known for her teaching abilities. In fact, the whole family was gifted, and Mary Riley would often be part of the various conferences that were held in the state of California.

Rachel set the dictionary down and started preparing the next lesson for youth group. It was time to start teaching the teens of her church what it means to have purpose in life. Tapping her fingers to her lips, Rachel pondered how to get them excited about life beyond their teenage years.

She was deep in thought when the sound of voices interrupted her concentration. Pausing for a moment to listen, she recognized her mother's voice, but the other one was new. Forgetting her lesson preparation, Rachel followed the sounds until she found her mom and the source of the unknown voice. What she saw as she entered the kitchen was a sight she had seen repeated over and over as she grew up. There, standing in her mother's immaculate kitchen was a large man. From the looks of his threadbare clothes and their lack of being laundered in a long time, it was apparent that the man was homeless.

"Now look at the mess on your floor, Ma'am, I told you my shoes were too dirty." His words were filled with shame and Rachel almost winced as compassion filled her heart. She wasn't the least bit surprised to see her mother reach out and pat the man's arm.

"It's all right. Nothing a little soap and water can't fix." Mary had already prepared the man a large sandwich and was placing some bananas and apples in a bag next to the plastic-wrapped tower of meat, cheese and bread. With her trade-mark smile that matched the size of her gentle heart, Mary sent the man off with words of God's love and blessing.

Without a word, Rachel picked up a rag and knelt down to clean the floor. Maybe she should make that youth lesson about loving others instead.

* ◦ ● ◉ ● ◦ *

The last few years had been completely different for Frank Smith. While Rachel was growing and blossoming, becoming successful in her endeavor to follow God's plan for her life, Frank was anything but successful.

After an ugly break up with his girlfriend, he had moved to a big city, filled with excitement and anticipation of a better life. But here he was, living in a dilapidated apartment. His new job included a difficult boss and he hadn't saved any money either. It looked as if he were doomed to keep living the same way he'd lived for the past twenty-five years.

Depression crept its way into his life and each day it got worse. He was constantly reminded of his failures. It seemed as if his dreams of being rich were drifting farther and farther away. And each time he was down, he would go to the bar. While the beer would chase his blues away for a short time, they always came back and he'd done nothing except spend money. And wasn't it a lack of money that made him depressed in the first place?

So once again, Frank packed his few belongings into his old beat-up truck and drove away. Hoping to leave his old life behind, he went in search of the new one he'd been dreaming about. This time, he decided to go live with his brother. Even though he and Phil hadn't had the best relationship in the past, Frank was hopeful that he was making the right choice. Besides, at this point, he had nothing to lose.

* ◦ ◦ ◉ ◦ ◦ ·

When Frank had walked over and talked to the lady feeding the neighbor's dog, it was out of pure curiosity. But now he was wondering if it was karma or good luck. The lady, who introduced herself as Ruth, was related to the family and it didn't take long for Frank to see that she was very proud of them. The fact that she carried their picture in her pocket spoke not only of her love for them, but also of her loneliness.

"Isn't that just the nicest picture?" Without asking him if he wanted to look, she handed it to him.

Frank gave her his best smile. He couldn't believe his luck. Phil had told him the couple who lived across the street had a daughter; but he hadn't mentioned she was so pretty. "It sure is, Ma'am."

"Oh, I miss them when they're traveling! I get so lonely for them even though they aren't gone for very long." Ruth looked like she was about to cry. "That's why I come here every day. Just seeing the house and taking care of their dog makes me feel closer to them somehow."

"Well, Ma'am, I'd be happy to sit a while and keep you company."

"Oh, you're such a nice young man!"

They sat out on the front porch and talked for a long time. With just a few smiles and a little bit of charm, Frank had easily become a friend to Ruth. After asking her many questions, Frank learned how her daughter's family represented the only relatives she had.

"I do have a sister. Well, not really a sister, but she sure felt like one even though she was just my friend. Lucy and I lost contact long ago." She shook her head leaving Frank with the impression that she wished it weren't so. "You've been so sweet to talk to me all this time..." Ruth looked up at Frank with uncertainty in her eyes, "Can I tell you something no one else knows?"

With the same smooth and overly sweet smile, Frank said, "You can tell me anything."

After hesitating for just a second, Ruth began confiding in him. "You see, Lucy had a baby when she was just sixteen. In those days, it just wasn't heard of like it is now and it almost tore our families apart; the shame, the guilt, the gossip. I'm afraid I didn't help much because from that time on I started to distance myself from her. I didn't want people to think I was like her."

Ruth started to cry and there was silence as Frank tried to think of a way to keep her talking. The more information he had, the better his chances were at making this beautiful girl in the picture his girlfriend.

"It's ok, you can tell me. You'll feel better if you talk about it." Frank said in a soothing voice as he took her hand in his.

"Oh Frank, Lucy and I said some pretty horrible things to each other! It got so bad that we stopped talking altogether. I don't even know where she lives now. I don't know if she's dead or alive. How I wish I could make amends."

"What about the baby? What happened to it?"

"Oh, the baby was adopted by a nice family back East; I don't know what their names were. But I do know they named her Lucille, such a nice little name and so close to her mother's name. Wish I could see her face. Sometimes I wonder if she had kids of her own..."

Frank thought this was some of the most interesting information he'd heard in a long time. *What are the odds that my stepmom's name is Lucille? I wonder how many adopted Lucilles are out there...*

Chapter 2

Wrapping up a conference always brought a sense of satisfaction for Rachel, and after being on the road for a few days, nothing sounded better than going home.

"So Dad, what do you think we'll find when we get back?" Rachel asked one of her favorite questions while driving home.

"Well, you never really know. Hopefully it didn't rain too much while we were gone. I was hoping to get that hedge trimmed. It'd be hard to do if everything is all soggy." Dan Riley was watching the road ahead. It was late at night and Rachel was talking with him to make sure he stayed awake. These were some of her favorite times with her dad. While Rachel's mom slept, the two of them would talk. As late night conversations go, they never knew what they'd end up talking about.

"Well, I would imagine we need to get that done as soon as we can. Our coastal weather isn't going to be dry for much longer. Maybe we could do it tomorrow."

"That would be great."

The stretch of silence had been a little too long so Rachel said the first thing that came to mind. "I'm ready to hold Shadow."

"Yeah, that dog will be happy to see us! He's probably ready to be inside the house again."

Shadow was a stray Rachel had rescued when he was a puppy. The small Miniature Schnauzer was just a scraggly ball of fur when Rachel brought him home. But now, years later, he was healthy and fat.

"Do you remember the time your Grandma Ruth told us about? When Shadow got stuck on top of his dog house while we were gone?"

"Yes." Rachel started laughing so hard, tears came to her eyes. "I still can't believe he got up there, he's so fat!"

"I can't believe she had to ask the neighbor to get him down!" Dan was laughing just as much as Rachel now and he went on to tell her a funny story about his childhood. It was supposed to be related to the current topic, but in reality it was just a new version of a story he had told many times before. With each telling it got a little more outrageous and less believable, but definitely funnier.

The rest of the drive home was spent with small talk about the trip they had just finished and the things they would do once they were home. Thanksgiving and Christmas were the best part of the year in Rachel's opinion and she was excited the holidays were just a few weeks away.

For some reason, Rachel's mind wandered away from Christmas and focused in on how long she had been waiting for God to bring a man into her life. There were a few times when she met a handsome guy who caught her eye, but so far, she had made it to her twenty-first year without dating. God's plan for Rachel's life involved a lot of things, but casual dating wasn't one of them. She had wrestled and wrestled with God over that issue, but always at the end she had to agree with that still, small voice that told her to wait. And she was trying to patiently wait for God to bring the right person along, but some days it felt like she was going to end up an old maid. On those days she would talk to her friend, Violet. She was the closest friend Rachel had and, in many ways, she was like the sister Rachel had always longed for. Wishing she could call Violet, Rachel shifted her weight in the seat to get more comfortable and stared out the window.

As they pulled into the driveway late that night, Rachel noticed her neighbor had a new truck. With a yawn, she pulled her suitcase out of the trunk and stumbled her way to bed.

◦ ◦ ◉ ◉ ◦ ◦

She hadn't thought about the neighbor's new truck. People got new vehicles all the time. But the next day, Rachel found out it wasn't just a new truck—it was a new neighbor.

With Rachel's help, her parents had started the long task of trimming the hedge along their house. As they were hard at work, Frank made his way across the street to meet them. He talked more to her parents than to Rachel because she was a woman on a mission and that mission was to finish the hedge before lunch. New neighbor or not, she wasn't taking much time to talk.

Later that day, as Rachel was folding laundry while watching TV in the living room, her parents mentioned the new neighbor.

"Rachel, was there any reason in particular you were so rude to Frank?"

Rachel placed a pair of neatly folded jeans on a stack of clean pants and looked at her mom in surprise.

"Really? I didn't think I was being rude. I just had a lot to do."

"Well, Sweetie, you were being rude." Mary came over and started to fold the laundry with her daughter. It was a nice gesture and Rachel appreciated it.

"If you had hung around a little more, you would have heard him say we are practically related," Dan said.

"Practically related, what does that mean?"

"Well, you know how your mom's family doesn't talk much about the past?" Dan looked at his wife, Mary. "I guess your mom's mother had a friend she claimed as a sister. And that friend had a daughter no one knew about. *Aunt* Lucy was only sixteen and unmarried at the time, so her parents sent her away until after she had the baby. They were so embarrassed, and so was our family; they all swore the baby never existed. The daughter, who was named Lucille by her adoptive parents, married a man who had two boys. We've been living next to one of those boys for years now and didn't even know it. Frank said they didn't piece it all together until he moved in with his brother a few weeks back. Their stepmom had mentioned something about her biological family living on the coast of California when she was born. He said he started looking into it and just happened to meet your grandma the day before he found out."

"Whoa, are you kidding?"

"No, he's not kidding," Mary said with excitement. "It appears I have a first cousin I've never met. And that means you have two second cousins!" Mary reached out and put her hand on Rachel's arm.

"But he's only related through friendship and then marriage, Mom."

Mary shook her head. "That still counts and you know it! You should have been friendlier when he came to meet us. The poor guy is family and new to town. He probably needs some help making friends."

And so it was, Rachel had family connections she never knew about, and her parents were asking her to befriend one of them.

⚬ ⚬ ◉ ● ◉ ⚬ ⚬

Even though Frank was hoping to meet Rachel when he had walked over to meet his new neighbors, he felt completely unprepared when he met her. He was standing next to the car in the Riley's driveway, talking to Dan and Mary, when a petite brunette came around the corner of the house. Her arms were full of leaves and branches. At first she didn't see him because she was focused on maneuvering through the gate without dropping anything, but when she looked up, she stopped moving for just a moment. She looked right into his eyes and something happened inside him. The picture Ruth had shown him hadn't captured her right; it hadn't done justice to her. In the picture she was pretty; in person she was more than just pretty, she was captivating. Her hair was dark brown and her lips were full. And she had these hazel eyes that held innocence. He'd looked into enough women's eyes to recognize the hardness that accompanied the type he'd dated before and swore he'd never date again. This girl was different than any he'd met before. In the split second when their eyes met, he was convinced she was the girl he'd been searching for.

He felt a sense of loss when she walked away and continued working; he wanted to follow her and beg her to talk to him. And that's when he set his plan in motion. It was earlier than he had planned, but after meeting her, he didn't want to wait and he decided the sooner the better.

He could remember the twinge of guilt he'd felt as he lied to Rachel's parents. He felt bad about lying. In fact, he shuddered a little each time he thought about it. Feeling the need to tell someone, he sought out Phil and told him what had happened.

"You told them what?" his brother shouted when Frank finished the story. "Why in the world would you tell them we are connected to their family? And how in the blazes do you think they won't know the truth? All it will take is for Ruth to try and find her friend and the whole thing will blow up in your face."

"Ruth won't go looking for her. I told Dan and Mary that Lucy is dead." When Phil just shook his head, Frank continued pleading his case.

"I've got to know her. Rachel might be my only chance at happiness. I've got to make her love me! If they think we are long lost family friends, then maybe I can spend some time with them and I can get to know her." Frank's voice sounded desperate.

"Frank, that just might be one of the stupidest things I've heard in my life!" Phil was laughing at him now. "That girl won't look at you twice. She hasn't dated a boy yet and she sure isn't going to waste her time with you. She's one of those good girls. You know the type, saving herself for marriage and all that stuff."

Jealousy filled Frank.

"How do you know so much about her? Do you like her? Is that why you didn't tell me more about her? I see how you are, you can't have her and you don't want me to have her. You can't discourage me." Frank grew angrier by the second.

Phil held up his hands to calm his brother.

"Look, it's a small town and people talk. That's how I know she's not the dating type, that and the fact I've never seen boys hanging around her. You're ridiculous if you think I've got my eye on her 'cause I don't. I'm not trying to discourage you; I'm trying to tell you the truth. Girls like that don't get mixed up with guys like us."

"How do you know she's not going to like me?" Defensiveness always came quick, almost as quick as his anger.

"Well, what kind of girl wants a guy to lie to her? You still didn't answer my question. What makes you think they won't find out the truth?" Phil put his hands through his long dark hair. He was obviously grieved over what had happened and Frank was reminded that Phil hated deceit.

"Well, it sort of just all worked out, I didn't have to lie much." Frank told Phil the story Ruth had told him. He pointed out how the name fit their stepmother's name and how Ruth had lost all contact with Lucy. The only thing making it unbelievable that his stepmother was indeed Lucy's baby was how horrible a person she was. Frank never knew if it was being adopted by unloving people or the alcohol that made her so filled with hate. If he had known the reason she wanted to find her biological mother was to kill her, he never would have helped her. Phil was lucky, he didn't bear that guilt. He had kept to his strict rule of minding his own business and had refused to help in the search. Frank wished he could change history. And for Ruth's sake, he was glad his stepmom wasn't truly her Lucy.

"That girl's going to hate you when she finds out you lied. And I don't blame her."

"No, she won't. I have it all figured out. After she falls in love with me, I'll tell her the adoption agency called to say they gave me the wrong information. She'll never have to know I lied in the first place."

"Sure, just keep adding more lies. That's your plan? Don't count on me to get involved. It's your life, not mine. I won't tell, but I won't be there to pick up the pieces when this thing blows up in your face."

Phil had made his point. Frank knew his plan would be doomed if she ever found out. But now that Dan and Mary saw him as family, they might encourage Rachel to spend time with him. *Especially if I tell them I'm having a hard time getting connected to people and feel lonely. Maybe it's a long shot, but it might work. And just like I thought, Phil agreed not to tell them. Good old Phil, I can always count on you.*

Chapter 3

Rachel's next encounter with her newfound family friend was slightly more eventful, and a little unsettling. It happened when she had gone outside to wash her car. Not only had she made a name for herself by choosing not to date, Rachel owned a 1990 Ford Mustang. It was painted a deep cherry color which appeared either black or red depending on the light. It was a thing of beauty, and needless to say, she got a lot of attention when she drove it.

When Rachel decided to go out and wash her car, it had never occurred to her that she would have company, so she was a little surprised when she saw Frank come out of his house and walk straight towards her.

"Hey Rachel, washing your car I see," he said.

"Yeah, thought I would get all the grime off. It sure gets dirty in this ocean air."

As Rachel was filling the bucket with water, she took a minute to look at him a little more closely. He had dark hair which was closely cut, a round head and glasses. He had to be at least six feet tall. His arms were huge and she wondered for a moment how many hours he spent working out each day. His physical presence was a little intimidating to her. Rachel was just barely above five feet and while she was muscular and fit, she felt very small next to him.

"I was watching for you, hoping you'd come out today so I could talk to you."

Rachel's mind quickly went from thoughts of his muscles and focused on what he'd just said. "Really? You've got nothing better to do than look out the window, waiting to talk to someone you barely know?" Rachel probably was a little rude, but there was something odd about the statement he'd just made and the way he looked at her caused a little quiver of discomfort.

"Well, I am waiting to hear back about the job I interviewed for, so other than waiting for the phone to ring and going to the gym, there's not much else to do."

Rachel saw her chance and seized it.

"You probably should go back in the house then. You wouldn't want to miss your phone call." Knowing she had practically told him to go away, Rachel added a small smile to soften the abruptness. After all, her parents had told her to be nice to the guy.

· ⊙ ◉ ◉ ⊙ ⊙ ·

"Oh, Violet! I'm so happy for you, but I'm going to miss you." Rachel said as she helped Violet pack her suitcase.

"I'm excited, but sometimes I get a little nervous." Violet grabbed a pair of socks and tossed them onto her bed. "I've never been to Mexico and I'm not too sure about working at an orphanage. What if the kids don't like me? So much depends on how well this trip goes. If they like me, they'll sign me on full time."

"That would be so awesome! Your dream of being a missionary would be coming true! Of course they'll like you, Vi. How could they not? You're sweet and kind and you smile a lot. And, you have a nice nickname." Rachel's eyes twinkled with mischief as she teased her friend.

"Oh dear, that's one thing I'm not going to miss! I'm glad you won't be there to teach the kids to call me Vi."

Laughter filled the air as the girls teased each other. Violet continued to find items she needed for her missions trip and Rachel carefully placed them in the suitcase.

"You're lucky I'm here to help you, Vi. I can pack a suitcase like no one else!"

"Yeah, but how am I going to get it all back in there when I'm ready to come home? Do you plan on packing yourself in there too?"

"Ha-ha, I guess you'll just have to learn how to be less messy!"

"Oh, you are terrible! If I traveled as often as you do, I'd be good at packing, too," Violet said as she punched Rachel in the arm.

"Ouch! No wonder the boys run from you! Not only are you gorgeous, brilliant, and wise; you're violent! If that won't scare them off, I don't know what will."

"You're real funny, Rachel." Violet tried unsuccessfully to contain her laughter.

"Well, I bet Mr. Right is sitting at the orphanage, just waiting for you to come to Mexico. And he'll be a real man who's not scared of your punches!"

As Rachel continued to giggle, Violet pretended to be offended and stepped farther into the closet to hide her laughter. With clothing muffling the sound, she missed what Rachel said next. Certain it was another comical comment, she asked Rachel to repeat what she said.

"I said, speaking of guys, I wish you could meet this Frank guy."

Violet stepped out of the closet and sat down next to Rachel.

"I really need someone to give me a non-biased opinion of him. My parents think he's just lonely and needing a friend. But Vi, he seemed creepy the other day."

"What happened?" Rachel had Violet's full attention now.

"Well, not much really. But I was outside washing my car and he walked over to talk to me. Just as I was looking at how huge his arms are, he says he was watching for me." Rachel shrugged her shoulders in uncertainty. "Have you ever felt that something was wrong but you just can't put your finger on what it is?"

"Of course I have, many times."

"Well, that's how I feel. There was something about the way he looked at me... I can't explain it. But don't you think it's odd that he was waiting for me to come out of the house so he could talk to me? Besides, do you normally tell people those kinds of things?"

"Well, maybe he's really bored or lonely. What did your parents say about it?"

"I didn't tell them," Rachel said with a sigh.

"Why didn't you?"

"It just didn't seem like much to tell. What am I supposed to say? That I have no idea why, but Frank makes me nervous?"

"Maybe you should try and stay away from him. And if something else happens, you really need to talk to your parents."

"I know..." Rachel returned to artfully stuffing the suitcase. Why did she feel so uncertain about Frank? It wasn't as if he'd said something inappropriate. And she'd dealt with all kinds of guys in her travels. Some of them were really weird and she was always able to deflect their attention without feeling bothered. But those guys didn't live in her neighborhood. And the only contact they had with her was either during the conference or through mail. This was different; different enough to leave her unsettled.

Later that afternoon, Rachel walked into the kitchen where Mary was preparing dinner.

"Mom, I really want to make some cookies for Violet. She leaves tomorrow and I thought it would be nice for her to have something to munch on while they drive to the airport."

"Ok, but I think you'll need to go to the store, I just used all the butter."

"And I used all the brown sugar in my oatmeal this morning." Rachel looked through the cupboards, taking note of the things she would need.

"Do I have time to go now? Or do you want me to wait until after dinner?"

"That's fine, Sweetie, you can go now. And that way you can get some milk for the mashed potatoes."

"Ok, I'll try to hurry," Rachel said as she grabbed her purse and keys and ran out the door.

· ◦ ◦●◦ ◦ ·

Frank Smith was just hanging up the phone with the gas company when he saw Rachel get into her car and drive away. He was thrilled to know he got the job and seeing Rachel only added to the excitement he felt. *I'm going to tell her I got a job!* With that thought running through his mind, he grabbed his keys.

He had to force himself to slow down; otherwise he would have run to his truck like the house was on fire. How could one little woman get him so worked up? When he got into his truck, he put the keys into the ignition and started the engine. He shifted into drive and pressed the gas pedal to back out of the driveway. The truck lurched forward and he let out a curse while stomping on the brake as fast as he could.

"I'm so worked up I don't even know what gear I'm using..." he mumbled. He had come within inches of plowing through his own house. Wouldn't Phil love that!

His stubborn brother was still angry at him for lying to the Rileys and he certainly didn't need to give him more reasons to be angry. It would be horrible if Phil kicked him out.

After placing the vehicle in reverse, Frank backed out of the drive and made his way down the street. *This would be a lot easier if I knew where she was going.* But thankfully the town was small and there weren't too many places to look.

By the time he found her car in the grocery store parking lot, she was pulling out of her parking space. He was too late! He decided to just follow her to the next place she was going. Of course, he would have to be careful so she didn't notice. He wouldn't want her thinking he was weird or something.

It didn't take long for Frank to realize she was simply going back home. For fear of her knowing he was following her, he took a different route and pulled into his drive just minutes after she pulled into hers. She was just now opening the trunk to get her groceries. He had to hurry, this was his only chance.

"Hey, neighbor!" Frank called as he stepped out of his truck.

Rachel turned and looked to see who was talking to her. When she saw him, she gave a quick wave and turned back to her groceries. As she was pulling out the first bag, Frank walked up next to her and reached for the other one.

"Let me help you," he said, settling the paper bag into the crook of his arm and closing the trunk.

"Thanks." She refused to look at him.

Why is she being so quiet? How can she get to know me if she's always in a hurry to leave?

"So I got the job I interviewed for." Frank couldn't help the boyish grin that spread across his face.

"That's nice, I'm glad for you." Rachel finally looked at him. And when she did, those hazel eyes seemed to steal all his common sense away.

"You, uh… you sure are looking good today."

Frank didn't even realize what he had said until Rachel's whole attitude changed. Her eyes went from almost friendly to ice cold in a matter of seconds. He could think of a lot of names to call himself, but he decided to focus on salvaging the conversation instead.

"So, uh… you making dinner or something?" he stammered.

"No, my mom's doing that." Rachel bit off each word as if forcing herself to talk to him. Then a gleam lit her eyes and she turned to him, looked him full in the face and said, "Actually, I'm baking cookies for someone special."

And with that, she took the bag from his arm and walked away. As the screen door slammed, Frank wondered what had just happened. Most girls were flattered easily and would have loved the compliment, even if it was clumsily said.

As he pondered how to handle Rachel and win her heart, he walked to his own house. He was walking up the steps to his front porch when something hit him.

"Someone special?" He practically yelled the words. Did he have competition?

"Violet, the guy told me I looked good!"

"Oh my, I guess your funny feeling about him was right. Didn't you say he's ugly and smells like beer and cigarettes? Gross!" Violet stood in her doorway holding the cookies Rachel had stopped by to give her.

"My thoughts exactly."

"Well, you have to promise to tell me how it all turns out. By the time I get back, I'm sure he'll just be another humorous story to tell. It's not like you haven't dealt with guys being infatuated with you before."

"I haven't had to deal with a neighbor before, Violet. And laugh all you want, this isn't funny to me. Maybe it will be when it's all over with, but in the meantime, I have to go through that awkward conversation of explaining why I don't want to date a long lost family friend!" Rachel smiled as her last comment caused her to giggle.

"Well, enough with all this talk about Frank," Rachel said with a silly voice and a goofy expression. "Let's talk about you going to Mexico and finding Mr. Right."

"Whatever!" Violet laughed.

"Seriously though, Vi, I know God is going to do something great through you in the next couple of months. Who would have ever thought you'd be spending Thanksgiving with orphans this year? They will be so blessed to have you there."

With that, the two girls hugged and promised to pray for each other. Rachel said her goodbyes as she walked to her car and Violet stood in the doorway, waving until her friend was out of sight. *God watch over us both...*

Chapter 4

Shadow came running as Rachel stepped into the fenced area of the yard. He was eager to see her and Rachel absentmindedly wondered if he was happier to see her or the food she held in her hand. Setting the food down, Rachel knelt to pet his silky black fur. She continued to pet him while he ate and she talked to him the whole time. She told him he was a good puppy and every now and then he'd look up at her and bark. Rachel kept talking to Shadow until she heard the crunch of gravel beneath shoes. Suddenly feeling embarrassed about talking to a dog, her cheeks flushed as she looked up to see who was interrupting the conversation she and shadow were having.

"Oh, hi, Frank," Rachel said with a lack of enthusiasm.

"Hi Rachel, how are you?" Frank's voice held enough enthusiasm for both of them.

"I'm good."

"Are you ready for the holidays?"

"Yeah, it's my favorite time of the year."

"Mine, too, but I have a feeling this year will be the best yet." Frank's smile just about split his face in two.

"And why is that?" Rachel was just a little intrigued by his excitement and decided it wouldn't hurt anything to see what made him so happy.

"Oh, it's a surprise. But you'll find out soon enough. Once the New Year rolls around, everyone's holiday secrets are revealed."

"I guess that's true."

"Hey, I was wondering...now that the weather is colder..." Frank was suddenly jittery and Rachel had a feeling he was nervous. "I was wondering if you might want to get a cup of coffee with me."

As soon as the words were out, he sighed in relief. In fact, he almost seemed victorious. Did he think it was that simple? Just ask and she would say yes? Well, he could think again.

"No thanks, I'm not a coffee person." As she said the words, she bent down and picked up both the dog and the dish. Apparently, if she wanted time with Shadow, it would have to be in the house. Otherwise, she would have an unwelcome guest.

"It... It..." Frank just couldn't spit out the words. He took a deep breath and tried again as he followed her up the porch steps. "It doesn't have to be coffee!"

But it was too late; he was talking to the door she'd slammed in his face.

* • ◦ ● ◦ • *

Thanksgiving Day dawned crisp and cold but to Rachel, it was glorious. There was something so comforting about waking up early in the morning to the sounds of her mother preparing the big turkey and setting it in the oven to roast. The muted sounds from the kitchen on Thanksgiving morning always brought to mind a long list of things she was thankful for. Her growling stomach reminded her how grateful she was for a mother who knew how to cook. Thinking about those who would share their table today, she breathed a prayer of thanks for a family who opened their hearts and home to others. And most importantly, she was grateful for a God who provided not only her physical needs, but her spiritual needs too. Each year, Rachel's sense of God's goodness increased, filling her with gratitude for a Savior who was willing to die for the sins of the world.

As the day progressed, Rachel, Mary, and Grandma Ruth spent some quality time in the kitchen preparing the family favorites. Mary was busy making oatmeal rolls. The recipe had been passed down from generation to generation so many times that no one really knew who had started the tradition. Rachel got the yams out of the refrigerator and started peeling and cutting them. Just as she was peeling the last yam, the phone rang.

"I'll get it," Rachel said as she quickly washed and dried her hands. With the dishtowel still in her left hand, Rachel walked over to the phone and answered it.

"Happy Thanksgiving!" She said in cheerful greeting.

"Oh, ah… Happy Thanksgiving to you, too. Is Rachel there?"

"This is Rachel," she replied with curiosity. She couldn't recognize the voice and wondered who would be calling her.

"Oh, ah... good!"

"May I ask who this is?"

"Oh! It's Frank. And I just realized how many times I've said 'Oh'." He laughed. "I guess I was surprised to be talking to you already. Your voice is just as pretty over the phone as it is in person."

Rachel flapped her hands to get Mary's attention and when Mary looked at her, Rachel made a face that meant she wasn't happy about who was calling.

"Oh, well thank you," she replied, hating the fact that now she, too, was saying the word "Oh."

"No need to thank me for speaking the truth, Rachel."

"Um... well... I'm not so sure about it being the truth, but I guess we're all entitled to our own opinions."

"That we are. And that's the main reason I wanted to talk to you, Rachel. I'm of the opinion that the one thing I'm most grateful for this Thanksgiving is having you come into my life. You see, I was feeling really low until I met you. But then, when you smiled at me, I just knew life was going to get better. So thank you, Rachel, for putting the sunshine back in my life. I'm really grateful for that."

Rachel was so taken by surprise that for once in her life, she couldn't think of one word to say. Even if she had a dictionary in her hand right now, she was certain she wouldn't be able to find any words to properly express what she was feeling.

"Ok... I guess it's like I said, we're all entitled to our opinions... That was nice and all, but I have go. Have a great Thanksgiving."

With calmness she didn't feel, Rachel slowly hung up the phone and walked away. She had to take a moment to process what had just happened. She was seeking solitude, but her mother and grandmother had other things on their minds.

"Rachel? What was all that about?" Mary asked with concern.

"I don't really know, Mom." She just stood there, shaking her head.

"Well, who were you talking to?" her grandma asked.

"Oh, that was Frank. You know, the guy who lives across the street."

"And... " Mary was feeling a little alarmed, Rachel looked so shaken up.

"And he said I'm what he's most grateful for this Thanksgiving!" Rachel said as she nervously moved from one foot to the other. "He said I brought the sunshine back into his life!"

By this time, Rachel's voice had grown quite loud and agitated. She was loud enough to make her dad come investigate what was going on.

"What's the problem in here? You ladies get into a fight or something?" Dan joked. But as soon as he saw Rachel, he sobered.

"It's Frank," Mary said as she reached out and put her arm around Rachel's shoulders.

"What about him?" Dan was carefully looking at Rachel. "What happened?"

"Dad, he's just been saying weird things to me. First, he told me I was looking good when I saw him the other day. And now he just told me I brought the sunshine back into his life."

Dan sighed with relief. "Well, I don't see what there is to be so shaken up over. He's new in town, surrounded by people he doesn't know. He's probably just grateful to have a friend across the street."

The following conversation centered on reaching out to people who are alone on the holidays. Inviting Frank and Phil over for the Thanksgiving Day meal had been mentioned, but was never fully discussed as their first guest arrived in the middle of the conversation.

Rachel was glad for the distraction and took the opportunity to slip away to her room for a few minutes to think. Maybe her parents didn't understand what she was feeling. Honestly, she didn't understand her feelings either. All she knew was that she didn't want to be around Frank any more than she had to.

Chapter 5

With Christmas just a few days away, Mary and Rachel worked together in the kitchen making nutmeg cakes. Over the years, Mary had gotten into the tradition of making these moist, delicately spiced cakes for each of the neighbors. They wrapped the cakes in festive cellophane and went door to door, personally handing them out. It hadn't taken long for the neighbors to join the tradition and soon the cakes were traded for home canned jams and jellies or special chocolates and Christmas treats.

"Mom, we're almost done with the last cake! All I have to do is sprinkle it with powdered sugar," Rachel said as she placed the golden cake on a paper plate. "We need to hurry and get this done so I can get to the church. I have the youth Christmas party tonight."

"Ok, let's get started then. We'll go over to Phil and Frank's house first," she said with a satisfied smile.

"Awesome..." Rachel said with sarcasm.

"Now, now, let's try to be nice, ok?"

Mary walked out of the kitchen in search of her shoes and Rachel quickly dusted the cake with sugar and wrapped it. Knowing the cake was to be delivered to Frank, she dug around in the bag of bows until she found the ugliest one. *Might as well save the pretty ones for the others…*

Just as Rachel was thinking her defiant thought, Mary walked into the kitchen. Rachel's cheeks flushed with guilt and she turned her head so her mother didn't see. The unkind words echoed in her mind and she felt bad for being so ungracious. But as they walked up the steps to Frank's house, she decided she really didn't feel too bad about it after all, especially as more unkind thoughts came into her mind when he answered the door.

"Here's a nutmeg cake! Merry Christmas!" Mary said as she handed the cake to Frank.

Phil walked up behind Frank and smiled. "Thank you! I can guarantee this won't last until tomorrow. Bachelors don't get home baked cakes very often."

"Hi Rachel, did you make the cake? It looks really good." Frank looked at Rachel as he held the cake up to his nose. "It smells good too!"

"My mom and I made it." Rachel tried to put the emphasis on the word *mom*. But Mary didn't catch it and spoke up.

"She's just trying to be modest. We both worked on the cakes. But this one was indeed made by Rachel. She's such a good little cook!"

Rachel looked at her mom with a frown. What was her mother thinking?

The interaction with Frank and Phil was short and Rachel breathed a sigh of relief when the door had shut after they walked away. "Why in the world did you have to tell them I made the cake?"

"Don't be so dramatic, dear." Mary linked her arm in Rachel's. "Baking a cake isn't such a big deal. I bake and cook for people all the time."

· ● ● ● ● ● · ·

Frank and Phil sat at the dinner table with big slices of cake on their plates. Frank was grinning so big he almost couldn't chew.

"It was awful nice of Rachel to bake me a cake! She's a sweet little thing."

Phil choked on his cake. After some coughing and a drink of milk, he was finally able to respond to Frank's outrageous comment.

"I don't doubt that Miss Rachel is a sweet girl. But brother, I have to tell you, she didn't bake that cake just for you. It's a tradition. The Riley women bake cakes for all the neighbors every Christmas. If you looked out the window, you'd probably see Mary and Rachel taking cakes to other people right now."

"Think what you want, Phil, I know the truth. Didn't you see the way she was looking at me?" Frank stuffed half a piece of cake into his mouth. He closed his eyes in delight and then stopped chewing for a minute.

"Hey, Phil," he said, causing crumbs to fall out of his mouth. "I think this here cake has more than just spices in it."

"What in the world are you talking about now?" Phil grumbled.

"The cake, I think it has wine in it."

"Only a drunk or a good cook would be able to tell if a cake has wine in it or not. And we both know which one you are."

"Hey, you watch what you say!" Frank stood suddenly. He shoved his chair back and looked at Phil with anger. "I'm not a drunk. I haven't had a drop of liquor since I moved here and you know it!"

"Yeah well, two months isn't very impressive. Especially since you think Rachel is going to fix your life and you know she'd never abide you being a drunk. But I'll bet you anything that when you finally get it through your thick head that Rachel doesn't want to be in your life, you become a drunk again." Phil spoke with just as much anger. How many years had he dealt with his brother? How many times had he been fooled into thinking he'd change?

⋅ ∘ ◉ ∘ ⋅

It had been less than twenty-four hours and the cake was gone. Phil's prediction had come true. But the effects of the cake lasted even after it was consumed. Phil was wishing for more cake, but Frank was wishing for more attention from Rachel. And the absence of the cake only made it worse.

It was no surprise to Frank that he wanted to go talk to her. She had been in his dreams all last night. Those dreams were so vivid; vivid enough to make him feel like he had a deep relationship with her. He would have denied it with every fiber of his being, but he had allowed his mind to create an ideal person who didn't truly exist. And as a result, he was falling in love with Rachel Riley. But she was the Rachel in his dreams, not the real Rachel Riley.

With the boldness of a long-time friend, Frank walked across the street and right up to the Rileys' front door. After knocking several times, he decided to use the doorbell, too, just in case she didn't hear the knock. He knew she was home alone because her car was in the driveway and he had seen her parents drive away a few minutes ago.

As he stood there waiting, he rehearsed what he was going to say. It seemed like he was always tongue-tied around her and he was really hoping to do better this time.

Rachel opened the door but left the screen door securely closed and locked. *She's really smart, safety is so important. You never know who might be coming to the door. I'm glad she's so aware of danger; I wouldn't want anything bad to happen to her.*

"Hi Frank, do you need something?"

"I just wanted to thank you for that delicious cake," Frank said with a smile as he looked her up and down. She was in sweat pants, her hair was pulled up into a pony tail and she didn't have make-up on. She was adorable. It was exactly how he had imagined she would look like when she woke up in the morning.

"It was nothing, really. Mom and I do that every year for each of our neighbors." Rachel said with indifference.

She's so sweet. She doesn't want me to make a big deal about her doing something for me.

"So I was thinking, Christmas is almost here and I haven't got you a present yet." Frank's excitement was hard to contain. He was so anxious to buy her something. All the other girls he dated were always thrilled to have him buy them things and most of the time they thanked him in a real special way. Just the thought of it made his heart beat faster. A kiss was probably all she would give him, but a guy could hope.

"Is there something you want? Or do you want me to pick it out and have it be a surprise?"

"I appreciate the offer. It's real sweet. But I don't want anything. Please don't buy me a gift." Rachel seemed uncomfortable.

"I'd really like to."

"Thanks, but no thanks. Look, I have to go. I was in the middle of a... a project. Bye."

With nothing else to say, Frank said goodbye and walked home. So she didn't want him to buy her a gift... she sure was different! But that was just what he was looking for and the thought made him grin.

Chapter 6

Rachel woke early in the morning to the phone ringing. Since her bedroom was upstairs in the converted attic, she stayed in her warm bed and listened as her mom answered the phone downstairs. Mary's voice was sleepy and hushed as she greeted the caller a good morning, but moments later there was nothing sleepy or hushed about Mary's voice.

"Of course we'll be praying... I'm so sorry... I understand... I'm so sorry... Ok, I'll tell Rachel."

Rachel had an awful feeling in the pit of her stomach. Something bad had happened and for some reason, she just knew it had to do with Violet. Pushing her feet into her slippers and shrugging into a sweatshirt, she hurried down the stairs. She arrived on the landing just as Mary was hanging up the phone. Mary turned around to look at Rachel and broke into tears.

"Oh, Sweetie, Violet's been kidnapped!" Mary said through her tears.

"What? How could this happen?" Rachel was numb.

"Her mom didn't have many details, but she said the pastor of the orphanage was supposed to take her to the airport today but she never came to his office. After waiting a few minutes, he thought maybe she had forgotten or something and went to look for her. They never found her, Rachel. All her things are still in her room, packed and ready to go. They found her shoe in the street, there must have been a struggle."

"No, this can't be happening!" Rachel broke into sobs as she ran back up the stairs. Sorrow and fear washed over her in waves that threatened to drown her. She flung herself across her bed and sobbed as her mind was filled with all the terrible things that happen to people who are kidnapped. When her eyes were swollen from crying and her throat ached from sobbing, she decided it was time to do something that would actually help Violet. She started to pray. Rachel had heard of intercessory prayer before, but she had never really thought much about it. But that cold December morning, safe in her little room, she prayed like she had never prayed before. And while Rachel's only thought was for the safety of her friend, the words of her prayer would stay with her for years to come, impacting her just as much as her friend.

* • •●• • •

Rachel didn't even know she had fallen asleep, but a few hours later, she jumped as she once again was awakened by the phone. This time she didn't just wait and listen for her mom to answer the call. She was downstairs and reaching for the phone before her mom was able to answer it.

"Hello?" Rachel said, desperate to hear news of Violet.

"They found her!" Violet's mom, Cora, was crying.

"Praise the Lord! Is she ok?"

"She's fine. I don't know any details yet, we're waiting on a call for that, but I do know she's ok and she's on her way home right now. Her plane will land late tonight."

"Tell her I love her and I'm glad she's ok, will you?"

"Of course I will. I'm worried I'll miss the call. I have to go!"

As Rachel hung up the phone, she once again sunk to her knees in prayer. This time she was surrounded by her parents and they all prayed together, prayers of thanksgiving for God's protection and mercy.

· ∘ ● ◉ ● ∘ ·

Christmas was still a few days away, but Rachel felt like she had already received the best gift she could ever get. Violet was home and she was safe. Sitting in her best friend's car as they drove to the beach, Rachel prayed and thanked God for her safety.

"Violet, what really happened in Mexico?" Rachel decided it was time to actually ask. They had been together for a few hours already and Violet hadn't said one word about it.

"Rachel, I just don't want to talk about it. I didn't listen to what I was told. They specifically told me I wouldn't be safe if I went to that part of town. But I went anyway, knowing I was disobeying. I deserved what happened. It was my fault and I don't want to talk about."

"Ok, but you can't keep it in forever, you know."

"Now you sound like my parents. They said I would have to get counseling if I didn't share with them what happened."

"Well, I don't think that's such a bad idea, Vi. Those types of things need to come out so they don't keep hurting you. Plus, people need to know that visiting the orphanage wasn't what put you in danger. What if I want to take the youth there sometime? The parent's need to know it's safe." Rachel looked at her friend, but Violet was too focused on the road to look her in the eye. "I know you're here and you're safe now, but did anything happen? Are you really ok? I care about you."

Violet took her focus off the road for a split second to look at Rachel. There were tears in her large brown eyes as she said she didn't want to talk about it.

Rachel hurt for her friend. For now, there was nothing she could do but pray. She wouldn't ask again, Violet would talk about it when she was ready.

"It's hard to believe that Christmas is just two days away. Are you going to the Christmas Eve service at church tomorrow?" Rachel decided to change to subject.

"I'm going. I'm looking forward to it. I always like the candlelight service." Violet smiled for the first time today; a small wistful one, but a smile nonetheless.

"It's always so pretty and our sanctuary is perfect for it with all the windows with wide sills. You know... a candlelight wedding would be beautiful in our church, too. Did you meet Mr. Right at the orphanage?" Rachel couldn't resist bringing the joke back to life.

"Well, there were a lot of nice guys there, but I seriously doubt I caught the eye of any of them," Violet shrugged.

"Why would you say that?"

"Because I'm quiet and I'm shy. I don't wear flashy clothing and I rarely wear make-up. I'm not exactly the type to attract a lot of attention."

Rachel looked at her friend. This didn't sound like her. Violet was always the one telling her to be true to herself and not worry about what others thought. They had talked quite a bit about clothes and make-up and Violet always seemed comfortable with her choice of clothing and lack of make-up. *Someone must have said something while she was gone.*

"Yeah but when Mr. Right comes along, he'll be dazzled by your natural beauty. You don't need all that other stuff Vi, you're perfect the way you are." Rachel tried to encourage her friend.

"You're right; if I can't be me, then I don't want the guy."

"You could say that again!" Rachel laughed as she remembered her high-school crush. If she had been willing to change, he might have given her a chance. But that was before she'd surrendered to God's call on her life. She didn't want him anymore and she was certain that if she looked up the word "grateful" in the dictionary, it would have her name for the description. How many times had she prayed a prayer of thanks that she didn't go down that road? Even though she was still single, she was being true to herself and she would never regret that.

"Hey Rachel, speaking of guys, how are things with your family friend?"

"You'll never believe the things I have to tell you!"

The girls arrived at the beach and sat in the car to look at the stormy waves of the ocean. It was too cold to be out walking, but they still enjoyed the roar of the crashing waves. And as always, they weren't lacking for things to talk about.

· ◦ ●◉● ◦ ·

The decorations for the Christmas Eve service were beautiful and Rachel looked forward to spending time in worship. There was only one thing that took away from the beauty of the night—the arrival of a certain man named Frank.

Violet and Rachel were already seated and talking in hushed voices with the kids in the youth group when Frank walked in. It was only a few minutes before the service was to start and he quickly took a seat in the far back. Rachel felt the air rush out of her when she saw him. When she recovered, she tapped Violet's arm and whispered to her friend.

"Don't look now, but Frank just walked in. He's sitting in the far back."

Violet waited a small amount of time before she slowly scanned the crowd as if she were looking at the decorations. She smiled greetings to fellow church members and let her eyes linger on Frank for only a second.

"That real big guy in the back with the close cut hair?" Violet whispered back.

"Yeah, that's him. I can't believe he came! I guess that's a good thing, right?"

"I suppose it depends on why he's here." Always practical, Violet hit the nail on the head. If Frank was truly there to worship God, then it would be a good thing. But if he was there because of Rachel, it was a whole different story.

"Well, I'm not going to ask him why he's here, that's for sure. So I guess I'll just have to hope he's here for the right reasons."

"Well, try not to think about him. Don't let him ruin your night, ok?" Violet gave Rachel a small hug as the service began.

It didn't take long for Rachel to get lost in the familiar sounds of Christmas Carols. She was grateful she was simply part of the crowd this year. While she loved to participate in special events, there was something grand about sitting in a pew rather than being part of the service. It was her time to be ministered to, and she was going to soak up every part of it. She was so wrapped up in the service, she completely forgot about the man in the back row who watched her just as intently as if she were the one on stage.

Frank Smith was still reeling from the Christmas Eve service. The whole thing was different than he was expecting. First of all, the room had been lit by candles. Frank didn't know why, but he was surprised by that. Someone had taken great care in decorating the high-ceilinged sanctuary; there were red ribbons and green pine boughs everywhere. The storm outside that left rain streaming down the windows added coziness to the evening, making it seem even more special.

But what had surprised him the most was the service itself. There was nothing glamorous about it, but it had impressed him anyway. He'd never seen people so sincere. And there was such a sense of peace, a type of peace he'd never felt before. Sitting in the back pew, he realized that he'd been looking for this feeling his whole life.

Then, when he had glanced at Rachel during the singing, he understood what was going on. Rachel had led him here. She was the reason he felt so at peace.

Christmas came and went and the Rileys were preparing for the next event at the church. For Rachel, New Year's Eve arrived too quickly. She had a lot of planning left to do. She had decided to try something different this year and had contacted all the youth leaders in the area to put together a New Year's Eve Party. Her dad was going to do a special service, then she and the other youth leaders were going to lead the youth, and anyone who wanted to stay, in games and activities until midnight.

Glancing at the clock, Rachel realized she didn't have much time until she needed to be at the church. If she was going to be ready for this event, she needed to get going! Time was quickly passing and she had to start preparing the games for tonight.

Rachel pulled into the church parking lot at 5:52 that evening. She quickly parked and turned off the headlights. Grabbing her purse, she stepped out of the car.

She actually heard his truck before she saw it and groaned as she thought about Frank being there. *He is way too early! The service doesn't start for another hour!*

As Frank drove past her, he waved and smiled. For fear of being rude, she waved back and offered a polite, yet reserved, smile. Not wanting to be stuck in the parking lot with him, she hurried into the church.

As soon as she entered the big room that served as both foyer and fellowship hall, she began looking for Violet. Violet was in charge of the snacks tonight and had been at the church for a half hour already. Once Rachel spotted her blonde-haired friend, she walked toward her as fast as she could.

"Violet!" Rachel said to get her attention.

Violet turned to look at Rachel and held up a finger. She was in the middle of measuring out the lemonade mix. Rachel impatiently waited for her to finish counting.

When she was done, Violet looked at her friend and noticed how agitated she was.

"What's wrong?"

"He's here. What if he tries to sit next to me? What then? I don't want to sit next to him! Then he's going to stay after, I just know he is! I have a job to do! He can't be hanging around me the whole time. What am I going to do?" Rachel talked so fast, Violet barely understood what she was saying.

"Whoa. Let's take one thing at a time. Okay? Are you sure he's here?"

"Yes, he drove up as I was getting out of my car. He waved and grinned at me," Rachel said as she grabbed Violet's hand.

"Rachel, does this guy scare you?" Violet was serious, almost angry as she asked the question.

"No, he makes me uncomfortable, but I wouldn't say I'm scared of him. If I can just avoid him it would be so much easier."

"All right, that makes sense. But if he scares you, even just the littlest, you've got to tell your parents. Do you promise?" When Rachel hesitated, Violet took Rachel by the shoulders. "I'm serious. You can't be too careful."

"I will. I promise." Rachel looked into Violet's eyes and saw fear. *What happened to you in Mexico?*

"The next thing we need to do is find a seat and make it so he can't sit next to you when the service starts."

"Ok, I have to go to my office and finish up a few last minute things. Do you mind coming to get me when the other youth pastors start to arrive? I think there will be only two or three," Rachel said as she started to walk away.

"Wait Rachel, I don't know who I'm looking for!"

"Oh, that's right. Okay, just come get me when people start to show up. That will be better."

* * • ◉ • * *

Rachel was all ready for the service and the activities afterwards. She still had a few minutes to spare, so she sat at her desk and prayed for the evening. There would be a lot of unbelievers there tonight and she wanted to spend time praying for the message of Jesus' gift of salvation to be loud and clear. Ministering to the youth of Mendocino County had become her passion and she prayed that, someday soon, there would be more believers than non-believers representing the next generation.

A soft knock interrupted her prayer. Looking at her watch, she saw it was almost time to start. Rachel stood up and walked to the door just as Violet was opening it.

"Oh, sorry, I didn't mean to interrupt. I just got worried when you didn't answer right away."

"That's ok, thanks for coming to get me. I lost all track of time!"

Rachel and Violet took a few minutes to talk to the other youth pastors before the service started. While Violet was not on staff, she was one of Rachel's best volunteers, so Rachel always made sure she introduced her to everyone.

"Violet, come with me. I think that's the new youth pastor from Fort Bragg Baptist." Rachel motioned in the direction of a handsome young man. As the girls were walking toward him, Violet looked at Rachel and raised her eyebrow.

"Did you know he was so good looking?" she whispered.

"Shush, he'll hear you!"

At first, the man didn't notice Violet and Rachel as they approached him. He was deep in conversation with a teenager from his group. But when he turned her direction, he smiled and held out his hand.

"You must be Rachel Riley. I've seen your photo on the website for the youth conference next month," Jacob smiled.

"And you must be Jacob Grayson. I'm so glad you could make it tonight." Rachel shook Jacob's hand and noticed he had a firm grip. Rachel introduced Violet, and when they were done greeting each other she said, "You have a nice sized group with you tonight. Mostly girls..."

"Yes, we do. I think they're finally getting used to me," Jacob laughed as if he'd told a joke. "So can we sit anywhere we want?"

"Go right ahead and make yourselves comfortable."

Rachel was just about ready to say something else when Violet tugged on her arm. Excusing herself, she turned to hear Violet's urgent whisper.

"Rachel, Frank is coming out of your dad's office right now; I guess your dad was talking to him. Anyway, we better hurry and get a seat where he can't sit next to you."

Violet grabbed Rachel's hand and tugged her toward the sanctuary. The girls were almost into the sanctuary when Frank appeared at their side.

"Hi Rachel, it's nice to see you tonight. Who's your friend?" He asked as he winked at her.

"Oh, this is Violet."

Frank held out his hand and Violet reluctantly took it. After shaking Violet's hand, Frank held open the door to the sanctuary for them.

"May I sit with you lovely ladies?" Frank was pouring on the charm.

"We've already made other plans. I'm sorry." Violet surprised Rachel with her quick reply.

"Well, maybe next time then?"

Frank seemed disappointed, but Violet simply nodded her head and pulled Rachel down the aisle. Rachel was so stunned by what had just happened that she didn't have any time to respond, either to Violet or to Frank.

As she sat down, she couldn't help herself as she started to giggle.

"You sure handled that well. You had such grace and tact," Rachel whispered.

Violet gave her a smile and shrugged her shoulders.

The rest of the evening went better than Rachel could have hoped. Violet had managed to get Frank involved with the other youth pastors; the men were more than willing to take him under their wing when she told them he was not a believer. Rachel had to hand it to Violet, she had saved the evening. The ill feelings Frank caused Rachel to feel were still a secret between the girls. And even though Rachel hoped the whole problem would just disappear, she knew it wouldn't and soon she would have to tell her parents just how she felt about Frank, whether they agreed with her or not.

After bringing in the New Year with lots of noise and sparkling cider, the fellowship hall was cleaned and everyone started to go home. As Rachel was locking up the church building, Violet stood with her.

"That Jacob guy was nice. I think there's something to his name. It might be sign." Violet teased Rachel. "You know, the Jacob in the Bible loved Rachel..."

"Where do you come up with these things? Let's go home." Rachel laughed and said goodbye to her friend. They hugged and then walked to their cars.

Rachel started her car and put her seatbelt on. She turned on the defrosters to combat the humidity of the foggy night. Then for some reason she felt as if she were being watched, she glanced around and noticed that Frank's truck was still in the parking space next to hers. *I thought he left a few minutes ago.*

Rachel pulled out of the parking lot and headed home, looking in her rear view mirror every now and then. Sure enough, he was following her! Just when she was starting to get worried, it dawned on her. *Silly goose! He's not following you, he's just going home.*

With that thought, Rachel felt better and drove home without another look behind her. When she pulled into her driveway, she quickly turned off the headlights, set the parking brake and grabbed her purse. It took her a moment to insert the key into the door handle to lock the car. With a quick turn of her wrist, she heard the lock click, and she pulled the key out and turned to go inside. When she turned, movement across the street caught her eye and she noticed she was being watched. Frank had already gotten out of his truck and was just standing there, staring at her. He waved and smiled, like he always did when she happened to look his way.

She walked up to the front door and unlocked it. Against her better judgment, she looked behind her before she slipped inside. Frank was still there, waiting and watching.

It is after midnight, he's probably just making sure I got home safely. It's kind of sweet actually...

Chapter 7

"Rachel, we're so disappointed in you." Dan was admonishing his daughter the following morning. "We saw how rude you and Violet were to Frank when he walked into the sanctuary with you."

"I wasn't trying to be rude, Dad, but Violet just kind of took over and before I knew it, she told him he couldn't sit with us." Rachel said quietly, looking at the floor.

"Why would Violet be so rude to someone she just met? That doesn't sound like her. Or you, either. What happened?" Mary asked.

"Well, I told Violet how Frank has been hitting on me. You know, calling me pretty and wanting to buy me a Christmas gift." Rachel looked at her parents; then softly added, "And I might have told her I didn't want to sit next to him."

"Do you really think Frank is hitting on you?" Dan asked.

Rachel felt bolder now that her parents seemed to understand and said. "Yes, I do. And I have been trying to avoid him because I don't want him to ask me out. The last thing I need is to try and explain to him that I don't want to date him." Rachel rolled her eyes as if exasperated with Frank.

"I can't believe how conceited you are!" Dan's outburst caused Rachel to quickly realize that her father wasn't as open to her opinions as she thought. "That guy is practically your family. He's not a believer and we need to reach out to him," Dan continued. "Besides, surely you are mature enough to realize a Christmas gift does not mean the man is in love with you."

Rachel looked at her mom with pleading eyes, surely she would understand. Rachel had been accused of a lot of things, and unfortunately conceited was one of them. Since she had committed to waiting for her future husband, it seemed like the offers to casually date were more frequent. And every time she turned a guy down—no matter how gently—someone always seemed to be miffed. And the result was usually the same; Rachel was accused of being conceited and stuck up.

"I'm sorry you think that, but I just have a hard time believing his compliments and offers of gifts are simply one family member interacting with another," Rachel said softly as she made a mental note to look up the word "conceited" later. Maybe everyone was right...

"Well, I think Frank is probably just the type of person who notices things about people. He's probably lonely and just trying to be your friend. And Rachel, we know your personality can be a little... ah strong, when it comes to guys. Are you sure you're not overreacting?" Mary tried to defend Frank.

"I don't care about personalities. I care about what's right," Dan said.

"Dad, I care about what's right, too. What would you and Mom like me to do?"

Dan and Mary looked at each other. Mary raised her eyebrows and Dan shook his head as if in disbelief. Obviously, they thought Rachel should know the answer already.

"The right thing is to reach out to Frank and witness to him. He needs the Lord, Rachel."

"Ok, I understand what you're saying, but why me? Why is it my job? "

"Because you're single and you live across the street. And you're part of this family and this family reaches out to people," Mary explained. It made sense to Rachel and she started to think maybe she was wrong in her evaluation of the situation. After all, her parents were older and wiser.

"All right then, I guess I'll try and be nicer to him when I get back from Los Angeles." Rachel figured that working around the upcoming youth conference would give her a whole month to pray about it. And right now she was pretty sure most of her prayers would be for Frank to leave town while she was away, even though it looked as if he was here to stay.

"No, I think you need to go over today and make things right. You should ask him to go for dinner or something before you leave. Maybe take Violet along... You don't leave for another week. And you'll be gone for two weeks at the conference. That would be too long. When you know the right thing to do, you need to do it as soon as you can." Dan's statement caused Rachel's eyebrows to shoot up in surprise.

"You want me to go somewhere with him?" she squeaked out.

"Friends hang out all the time, you'll have fun. And don't worry; it's not going to affect your not dating thing." Mary tried to soothe her daughter. "And if nothing else, Violet will have the chance to make amends, too. We wouldn't want Frank to think Christians are rude."

* ∙ ∘●∘ ∙ *

With feet that felt heavier than concrete, Rachel reluctantly made her way across the street. Feeling much younger than her twenty-one years, she had insisted Mary come with her. *Sometimes you just want your mommy*, Rachel thought with a small smile.

When the two women reached the front door, Mary looked at her daughter and nodded her head, encouraging her to knock. With a shaking hand, Rachel knocked on the weathered door. *Get it together Rachel, there's no reason to be shaking.*

Phil opened the door and greeted them with a curious look.

"What brings you fine ladies knocking on my door?"

When Rachel just stood there, Mary decided she would have to take the lead.

"Well, we were actually hoping to talk to Frank. Is he around?"

"Yes, he is. He's got the day off from work for some reason." Phil frowned ever so slightly and Rachel wondered what was bothering him. "I'll tell him you're here. Why don't you come on in and sit while you wait?"

Phil escorted them to the table and offered them something to drink. When they both declined, he walked away to find his brother. The women waited for several minutes and just when Rachel thought maybe she was spared spending time with Frank, she heard some muffled talking. While the words were too muted to hear, the tone was clearly unhappy. Whatever the brothers were talking about, it was obvious they were disagreeing.

Moments later, Frank walked into the room with a smile plastered on his face.

"Mary, Rachel, it's good to see you!"

Mary looked at Rachel and this time her eyes were stern. It was a look that told Rachel she had better do her part. Rachel was starting to think bringing her mom wasn't such a great idea after all.

"So Frank, I was thinking… " She just couldn't do this! She looked at her mom again, hoping for mercy.

"Yes?" Frank said with a look of curiosity.

"Like I said, I was thinking… " Rachel had to clear her throat to keep going. "I'm thinking we should go get that cup of coffee you've been asking about." There, she'd said it. Now all she could do was hope that he'd say no.

"Oh, now that sounds great, but I'm just going to have to decline." Rachel couldn't believe her ears! She didn't think she could be any happier. "Yeah, I'll have to pass on the coffee because I would much rather go to that Mexican restaurant your dad was bragging on!" Frank was so excited.

"That would be perfect!" Mary added with enthusiasm.

Rachel's eyes were huge as she looked at her mother. Why in the world would she say that was a perfect idea? Rachel discreetly elbowed Mary and shook her head ever so slightly. If they went to that restaurant, they would have to drive to Fort Bragg. That was almost twenty miles!

"You know what would make it even better? We could go to a movie after we eat!" Frank was pacing the room now. He was so excited he couldn't stand still.

"Oh a movie…that would be, ah… " Rachel was trying her hardest to think of a polite way out of this rapidly growing problem.

"A movie would be great!" Mary agreed and received another elbow to the ribs. Looking at her daughter, she smiled and said. "I guess it's all settled then."

"Wonderful," Frank said with a huge smile. "I'll walk over to your place tomorrow around five. That should give us enough time to get there and eat before the movie starts."

All Rachel could do was nod her head yes and try to look more excited than she was. Once the plans had been started, they picked up speed faster than she could keep up with and as Mary waved her last goodbye, Rachel realized they had forgot to mention Violet would be coming as well.

· ● ◉● · ·

Frank could not believe what had just happened! Rachel came to his house to ask him out! He was so surprised. After the ways things went last night, he was certain it was going to take a lot more work to convince her to go out with him. But apparently, the plan was working! Mary was obviously encouraging Rachel to spend time with him. *Won't Phil be jealous when he finds out!*

When he thought about the way Rachel treated him last night at the church, he decided Violet must have influenced her. Rachel was a strong woman, but she must be equally loyal, too, because she had let her friend take charge of the situation. Rachel had probably wanted him to sit with them all along. And if he had questioned her about Violet's behavior, he was certain she would have defended her friend. That kind of loyalty was hard to find. Life was going to be great with that kind of woman at his side!

· ● ◉● · ·

Rachel had spent the rest of the day praying for God to make things okay. Every time she was reminded of the plans set for the next evening, she would get nervous all over again. Normally, she was a confident young woman who could read people as easily as she read her dictionary, but this situation just felt so different. She was so confused. She had looked up the word "conceited" and was certain the definition did not describe her. When she had grabbed the big book, she was almost hoping the word would fit her, because then it would mean that Frank really was just being a friend. But now, she was convinced she wasn't conceited and that meant either she had lost her ability to read people, or Frank really was hitting on her.

I hate this feeling… God, please let tomorrow go well.

· ○ ◉ ○ · ·

Rachel looked at the clock and sighed, it was 4:58. Frank would be knocking on her door any minute. After praying so much, she had felt better about the whole thing and had decided that her parents were right. There was nothing to worry about and she would probably have a great time. She was going to make the best of the evening, and she was determined to make her parents proud. But then, Violet had called her and told Rachel a long, detailed story that ended with Violet being unable to join her on the outing with Frank.

Rachel was deep in thought about how she could best witness to Frank and not freak out about going to dinner and a movie with him alone when he knocked on the door. She wasn't quite ready for the evening and still needed to put her shoes on, but Rachel went to answer the door anyway. She would invite him in and he could chit chat with her parents while she got ready.

Rachel pulled open the door and was greeted by a very dressed up Frank. He was at least three feet away and his cologne was still overpowering! If those things hadn't unsettled her, what she noticed next was just about her undoing.

He brought me flowers!

Chapter 8

Rachel awkwardly asked Frank to come inside and wait for her to finish getting ready. She succeeded in appearing calm, but inside she was screaming. As Frank sat down, Rachel closed the door with more force than needed and the whole house rattled as it slammed. Rachel couldn't seem to make herself turn around and look at Frank again. She did however, look at her parents. She wanted to yell, "I told you so!" but settled with just a glare.

For what seemed like the millionth time since she met Frank, Rachel took a deep breath and steadied herself. It was obvious that her parents, too, were taken by surprise. None of them had expected the flowers. Dan and Mary simply sat on the couch and stared at the roses in Frank's hand. There was a long span of silence as Dan and Mary were at a loss for words and Rachel was too angry to talk. Frank was the only person who didn't seem bothered.

"You probably should put these flowers in water, Rachel," Frank said as he held them out to her.

"Oh, right." Rachel forced herself to reach out and take the red roses. It wasn't a grand arrangement; it was a simple one with only two roses and some baby's breath. But they were still the first flowers she had been given and Rachel resented them. *I should've never agreed to this! Violet, how could you bail on me?*

As she found a vase and filled it with water, she heard her parents start talking with Frank. They talked mostly of things like the weather, but Rachel did notice a not-so-subtle remark about relatives watching out for each other. Dan was making sure Frank understood that his daughter's wellbeing was of utmost importance and he expected Frank to watch out for her the same way a father or brother would. Rachel breathed a prayer of thanks for a father who cared enough to scare some sense into the guy.

After delaying as long as she could, Rachel picked up her purse and keys. It was time to take charge; she may not like the situation, but at least she would be in control.

"I'm driving!" she said as she gave her mom a hug goodbye. Moving away from her mother, she reached out and hugged her father. As he pulled her close, she whispered in his ear, "Pray for me."

Then, without another word, she walked out the door. Frank followed her lead and went to stand by the car.

"I can't tell you how excited I am to ride in this little beauty." Frank slid his hand across the hood. "This paint job is incredible. It's hard to tell if she's red or black."

"What makes you so sure my car isn't a he?" Rachel felt on the defensive and couldn't stop the contrary words from leaving her mouth. *Why do I even care about something so silly! It's a car, not a he or she. Lord, please help me be nice...*

Rachel opened the car door and got in. She quickly noticed how small the bench seat felt with this huge man sitting next to her. If she didn't know any better, she would say he was sitting closer to her than necessary. In a desire to get some space between them, she placed her purse next to her on the seat. The barricade felt small and inadequate, but the action gave her strength. She could handle this, she just had to be strong and tell him how things were going to be!

As they drove away, Rachel decided to just get right to business.

"So, I have to say, I wasn't expecting flowers."

"You weren't? All women love flowers; I knew you would like them." Frank said with confidence.

"Well, it's just that receiving flowers makes me think of boyfriends and dating. I had just assumed we were on the same page. I'm sorry if you think this is a date, because it's not." The boldness filled Rachel with satisfaction and a sense of power. Why was she so worked up about this? *It's pretty simple really; no one can make me go on a date if I don't want to. All I have to do is tell Frank the truth and that will be the end of it.*

"Oh, wow. I'll have to remember not to bring you any more flowers," Frank laughed. "Call it whatever you want, I'm just glad to be hanging out with my friend."

"Good. I'm glad we got that taken care of," Rachel sighed.

* ◦ ◦ ◉ ◦ ◦ *

Frank looked up from his plate of food.

"You know, Rachel, you're a strong woman and I really admire that about you."

"Thanks, I guess. But really, I don't think I'm all that strong. I have to tell myself all the time that I can do all things through Christ who strengthens me," Rachel said before taking another bite of food.

"You're different than anyone I've ever met. Have you ever thought about becoming a pastor? You'd be great at it!"

"Well, I don't really know what to say to that. I think youth ministry is where God wants me. A senior pastor isn't something that would work... " Rachel laughed. "I'm certain that God wants me to marry a pastor anyway, so I think I'll just keep planning on that until He says otherwise."

"Well, I guess I have two things going against me. Not only am I just your friend, I'll never be the kind of man people want for a pastor." Frank seemed to be joking, but Rachel wasn't so sure, and she didn't get much time to consider his level of seriousness because he quickly changed the subject. "So, uh, how does a person go about knowing what God wants?"

"Well, I could give you the classic answer and tell you to read your Bible and pray." Rachel looked at him with a little gleam of mischief in her eye. "And while that is definitely the best advice I can give you, I have to tell you to be aware of other ways God speaks, too. Like using your own mouth..."

"What in the world are you talking about?" Frank asked with genuine curiosity.

"I'm serious! That's what happened when God told me I was going to be a pastor's wife. I had been talking to this lady after a conference my dad spoke at when all of a sudden I hear myself telling her I was going to marry a pastor!" Rachel laughed a little. "But we don't have time for that right now if we are going to make it to the theater on time."

"Tell me while you drive. You can't leave me hanging like that." Frank said as he escorted her out of the restaurant.

To Rachel's surprise, the rest of the evening was enjoyable. The movie they had picked was entertaining and the ride home was spent in friendly conversation. Rachel had been cautious to keep her purse firmly between them and reminded him from time to time that they weren't on a date; and she was certain the issue was resolved.

However; just as Rachel pulled her car into the driveway, Frank asked a question that proved her wrong.

"So were you telling me all that stuff about marrying a pastor just to make me jealous?"

"Was I what?" Rachel was dumbfounded.

"You know, are you trying to make me jealous by telling me you want to be with someone I could never be?"

"It has nothing to do with that, Frank." Rachel was having a hard time believing he was accusing her of purposely making him jealous. "Why in the world would you be jealous? We will never be more than friends. I'm just not interested in you like that and the only reason we are sitting in the same car together is because of our family connections.

"And I forgot to tell you, but Violet was going to come with us tonight but it didn't work out. Frank, I don't casually date. Let me make this clear, this is not a date."

"I know we're just friends, but why wouldn't I be jealous? Anyone who could potentially take your friendship away from me is cause for jealousy. I just met you and I want to keep you in my life. I'm not going to let someone like you just slip away from my life."

Frank sounded reasonable, yet there was something about his response that didn't sound normal. It was times like this when Rachel really wished she had more insight into the workings of the male brain; because to her female brain, what he just said sounded possessive and creepy.

"Well, like it or not, there will be other people in my life. And in just a few days, there are about a thousand people who are counting on me being very far from here." *And I can't wait to drive away and put some miles between us!*

"Sometimes life isn't fair I guess." Frank opened his car door and got out. As he started towards his own home, he looked back at her and said, "Well, goodnight, friend. I had a good time."

"Bye." Rachel hurried to get her belongings out of the car. She just wanted to be done with the night. In her haste, she dropped her purse and with an exclamation of frustration, she bent down to retrieve her scattered belongings. Grateful that Frank had already gone home, she took her time picking up the various things that had fallen to the ground. The day had been long and she was running out of energy. When she was sure everything had been found and replaced, she stood up, locked her car and started toward her house.

As she was walking, she felt a small prickle at the back of her neck. Unable to shake the feeling of being watched, she paused mid-step and dared to look at Frank's house. Sure enough, he was watching her.

Rachel couldn't get in the house quick enough. Running up the steps, she got out her keys and fumbled with the lock. *Keep it together Rachel, he's watching you. Don't let him know you're scared.*

After trying two times, the door finally opened. Filled with relief, she leapt inside, then slammed and locked the door. She wasn't sure how; but in her panic she ended up on the floor. Still breathing hard, she just sat there for a while and tried to calm down. She had no idea why she had been so scared. All she knew was that something inside of her was yelling at her to get in the house. Now that she was safe, she felt like crying.

Rachel was picking herself up off the floor when all of a sudden she remembered something.

"No, it can't be!" She gasped and sat back down. "This doesn't have anything to do with my prayer. It just doesn't!" Rachel repeated those words over and over, hoping she would believe them. She desperately wanted to believe them. But try as she may, she couldn't.

Chapter 9

For reasons unknown, even to herself, Rachel chose not to tell anyone what had happened with Frank. When her parents asked her how the evening had gone, she simply told them that she was able to witness to him and requested them not to make her do it again.

All she wanted to do was go on the road and not think about the problem for a while. And to Rachel's relief, being at the conference had given her just what she was hoping for. The time spent teaching fellow youth leaders took her full attention, leaving her with little time to worry about Frank.

Rachel had been surprised to see Jacob Grayson there. Most of the youth leaders from Mendocino County didn't make it all the way down to Los Angeles for the training offered there. It was a week-long event that took place at the beginning of every year. And each time she taught, she would challenge the youth leaders to make the New Year one of great growth and outreach.

"Hey Rachel! I was wondering if we could spend the break together," Jacob said when he met her in the lobby of the hotel that was hosting the conference.

"Oh sure, I think that would work out nice. It's good to see someone from home." Rachel smiled. "Let's grab some coffee." As the words left her mouth, she was reminded of the lie she told Frank. She really was a coffee person; she just hadn't wanted to spend time with him. *Lord, forgive me. And please, let me not think about him right now.*

After they purchased their coffee, they found a table in the corner of the lobby and sat down. Sitting across from Jacob, Rachel couldn't help but admire his looks. He had black hair and green eyes; it was a combination she had always liked.

"So I have been meaning to ask you something." Jacob smiled and leaned toward her in a friendly gesture. "How in the world did your family end up in a tiny town like Casper? With both you and your dad being so well known in the Association, I would have assumed you lived in a bigger city."

"It's quite simple, really; my dad was already pastoring at Casper Community when he started working with the Association. When he got his first book published, he started getting job offers from churches all over the state. Some of them were big, well known churches, too, but Dad loves his congregation. He said if it wasn't for them and the support they've given over the years, he would never be who he is today."

Rachel took a sip of coffee and noticed a book in Jacob's hand.

"What do you have there?" She asked with a twinkle in her eye.

"Oh, just some random book I picked up. I've never heard of the author before, do you think it's any good?" Jacob picked up the book and waved it at her.

"I don't know, with a title like that, it might be boring," Rachel laughed.

"Seriously though, I didn't know you had a book out. That's awesome. And here I thought you were just a terrific youth director."

"Well, Mr. Grayson, I'm one of those people who are full of surprises."

Jacob was just about to respond when they were interrupted by someone calling Rachel's name. They both turned to see who it was, and Rachel recognized the Association's Director of Youth.

"That's the guy who oversees anything youth related in the Association. His name is Bill Harvey," she whispered to Jacob, uncertain if he already knew who the man was.

With a smile, Bill walked up to Rachel and pulled a bright yellow envelope out of his pocket.

"The hotel manager told me this came for you in the mail yesterday." He looked at her and winked as if there was something special about the letter.

"Thank you," Rachel said as she reached out and took the letter. She quickly glanced at the return address and gasped when she saw the name written there. "It's from him," she whispered.

"What's that, darlin'?" Bill asked. He had known Rachel and her parents for about ten years now and had grown to love them as if they were his own family.

"It's from my neighbor, Frank," Rachel told him. Then she looked at Jacob. "Remember him? He was at the New Year's Eve Service."

"Yeah, I remember. I didn't realize you were that close." Jacob seemed surprised by the letter. "Aren't you going home in just a few days?"

"I didn't realize we were that close either," Rachel said as she stood up and excused herself from the conversation.

As she walked away, the two men looked at each other.

"What was that all about?" Bill asked.

"I have no idea... I'm Jacob, by the way. I'm the new youth pastor at Fort Bragg Baptist."

"It's nice to meet you, Jacob," Bill said as the men shook hands.

· ∘ ●◉● ∘ ·

Rachel looked around the hotel parking lot and found a nice shady spot under a tree. She bent down and touched the bright green grass, satisfied that it was dry, she sat down. *He must have sent this the day after I left,* she thought as she looked at the envelope in her hand.

Frank's penmanship was horrible and he'd spelled her name wrong. But what caught her eye was the postage stamp. With Valentine's Day around the corner, it made sense that the stamp said "Love." But Rachel couldn't help but wonder if it was chosen on purpose.

Turning the envelope over, she stuck her finger into the back flap. Pulling down on the seal, she ripped it open and took the card out. The front of the card had a picture of a black Miniature Schnauzer that looked like Shadow.

Rachel opened the card and quickly saw the words "Doggone it, nothing's the same without you" printed in bold, black letters.

And of course there was a personal message written under that. His messy handwriting had a strange mixture of upper and lower case letters; Rachel had never seen anything like it. He wrote:

"you are a beAutiFUL PeRSON.
I am LooKinG FOrwaRd to SHaRe LiFe wiTH.
LOVE FOreVER
FRANK"

Rachel could barely believe what she had read! This guy acted like he had a right to be saying he loved her! Apparently he hadn't understood her when she said they would never be more than friends.

Knowing it was time to go back and finish the conference, she stood up and tucked the card into her back pocket. *At least I still have three days until I have to deal with this.*

Chapter 10

Rachel woke up the next morning to the phone ringing. Knowing it was the wake up service the hotel provided, she almost didn't answer. But for some reason, she picked up the phone and was greeted by a cheerful voice.

"It's time to wake up, Miss Riley. And when you get a chance, stop by the front desk. There's a letter here for you."

Rachel thanked the lady and set about her morning routine. After preparing for her day, she left her room to get some breakfast. On her way to the hotel restaurant, she went and retrieved the letter she was told about.

This time it was a blue envelope, but the penmanship was still the same and so was the sender. Frank Smith. *Will I never be able to get away from him?*

Picking out a table near the window, Rachel ordered her breakfast and settled in to read the letter. With a mixture of curiosity and dread, she took the single sheet of lined notebook paper from the envelope and unfolded it.

"Dear Rachle,
I CAN NOT STOP THiNKiNG aBouT you and
The way you MaKe me FeeL. I HAVe NeVeR
feLT tHiS way aBouT anyone BeFoRe and I
Know IT's Because I LOVe You. You Have
Changed my LIFe mOre THeN you will ever
Know. THiNgs aRe Good WHeN you aRe
HeRe. You Make Me HaPPy and I KnoW I
Can'T Be THAt HaPPy WithOUt You.
I HAVe Been Going tO THe gym. I WanT TO
LooK Good For You.
I Need TO go STaRT SHoPiNg For YouR
valentine's giFTs. We Can HAVe Fun that Day.
Have a good TRiP. I can NoT wait to see you
aGain. God Bless you WHilE You ARE On
your TRiP.

LOVe FOreVer,

FRANK"

Before Rachel finished reading the letter, her hands started shaking. When she finally read it all, her pulse was racing and she fought to control her emotions.

Fueled by anger, Rachel forgot about her breakfast and ran to her hotel room. She unlocked the door and walked straight to the phone. With quick movements, she dialed the number she knew by heart.

"Hello, Riley residence," Dan Riley said when he answered the phone.

"Don't ever tell me I'm conceited again!" Rachel yelled.

. ◦ ◉⬤◉ ◦ .

Frank could barely stay upright on the bar stool. He swayed from side to side, but somehow managed to keep from falling off.

"Hey there buddy, I think it's time to call it quits." The bartender spoke the words again as he gathered up the empty bottles in front of Frank.

"I'm never calling it quits," Frank slurred, waving his hand and almost falling. "I'm never giving up on her. She's my mate's soul... soul mart?" Looking puzzled, he waved his hand again and said, "You know what I mean."

The bartender just looked at him and rolled his eyes. It was almost time to close and this guy wouldn't be able to get up and walk out the door. He needed to call someone.

"So, ah, is there someone you'd like me to call? You're too drunk to drive home, buddy."

"Did you hear what I said? I said she's the mate of my soul and I'm not giving up. It don't matter what she says."

"Ok, I hear you. Now, who can I call?"

"I know she sent me this letter, but she didn't mean it." Frank pulled a crinkled envelope from his pocket and threw it in the bartender's direction. "I bet that Violet girl told her to. Violet must be jealous of me. But that's not gonna keep us apart."

The bartender picked the letter up off the floor and tried to hand it back to Frank but Frank shook his head.

"No, you read it."

"Thanks, but I've got some work to do and I need to close up. Who can I call to come get you? Should I call the police?"

"I said read it! Read that there letter and tell me she doesn't mean it!"

For fear of Frank turning violent, the bartender looked at the envelope. When he saw the overnight postmark and read the name on the return address, his eyebrows went up.

"I can tell you right now that if the girl you're talking about is a Riley, you better just leave her alone."

"What's with everyone saying that to me?" Frank was angry now. He tried to stand up, but his legs buckled under him. He sat down, swayed for a few minutes, and continued yelling. "She's in love with me! She's just too loyal to her friend to tell me. She told me to leave her alone. But she don't mean it."

When the bartender just shook his head, Frank got angrier.

"Listen to me! When she gets home, I'm gonna show her that things are okay. She's just upset right now, but when she gets home... when she gets home she'll regret sending me this letter. But its okay, I forgive her."

When Frank tried to stand up again, he passed out. The bartender tucked the letter into Frank's pocket, then walked over to the phone and called the police. It was time to get this guy out of here.

• • ◦●◦ • •

"Frank! I told you this was going to happen." Phil was so angry he could spit. It was bad enough that he had to go down to the police station and pick up his drunken brother, but now he had to listen to all this nonsense about Rachel loving him.

Phil had finally been able to drag Frank into the house and get enough coffee into him to sober him up a bit.

"Now, go take a shower, you stink."

Frank didn't respond verbally, but he started taking off his clothes as he walked toward the bathroom. Muttering about the need for Frank to grow up, Phil went behind him and picked up the alcohol soaked clothes. They needed to be washed and he wasn't going to leave them until morning; his whole house would smell like a bar if he did.

With the water filling the washing machine, Phil dug in the pockets of Frank's pants to make sure they were empty before he put them in to wash. When he put his hand in the right back pocket, he felt a wadded up piece of paper. Not thinking much about it, he pulled it out, put it on top of the dryer and stuffed the pants in the washer. As he dropped the lid on the washing machine, it created a puff of air that caught the crumpled paper and sent it soaring through the air. When it fell to the floor, Phil stooped to pick it up and place it back on the dryer before leaving the laundry room. He was reaching out his hand toward the dryer when something caught his eye. The writing on the paper was feminine. Curiosity filled him and before he knew it, he was unfolding the paper to see who the note was from. *So this is why he's drunk. I knew this was going to happen!*

After reading the neatly written words, Phil walked into the living room with the letter in his hand.

"Frank, hurry up and get dressed. We have something to talk about," he shouted.

"You think you can boss me around? You always did think you were the boss of me. I'm getting dressed and I'm going to bed!" Frank yelled as he walked from the bathroom into his bedroom wearing a towel.

Phil gave him a few minutes to get some clothes on, and then he went into Frank's room. Whether Frank was drunk or not, this couldn't wait.

"I found this in your pocket," he said, holding up the letter from Rachel.

"Yeah, what about it?"

"I told you to leave that girl alone! You're not going to get anything but trouble if you keep bugging her."

Frank pulled his covers back and climbed into bed. Pulling the blanket up close around his neck, he turned his back to Phil.

"I'm not listening to you, Phil; you're just like all the others trying to keep us apart."

"All the others? I have no idea what you're talking about. From this letter, it seems to me that Rachel doesn't want you talking to her anymore. Look at the post mark, she even made sure it got here overnight, it was that important to her. Frank, you're not together! And she said…" Phil never got a chance to finish his sentence. Frank was so filled with rage by the truth Phil was speaking that he leapt from the bed and pushed Phil's lanky body against the wall. Getting right up into his face, he screamed, "You just shut up!"

"No, I won't. You better leave that girl... "

Again, Phil was stopped from finishing what he was saying. This time, Frank's fist smashed into his jaw. With a loud crack, he felt a tooth loosen, and then he started seeing stars. As darkness was closing in on him, he whispered the rest of his sentence. "Leave her alone, she's gonna hate you."

Chapter 11

The thought of being home filled Rachel with apprehension and as she drove away from the conference, she couldn't stop wondering what the future held. After sending Frank the letter telling him to leave her alone, she could only guess what he was thinking, but she was pretty sure things weren't over and that made her stomach turn.

Rachel pulled into her driveway late Sunday afternoon. It was almost February and the rains of winter were taking a break. The day was beautiful and sunny. With a few hours of daylight left, Rachel decided to start unpacking her car; the sooner she did it, the sooner she could relax.

Rachel was on her second load when she noticed Frank was in his yard washing his truck. He had a stereo blasting and was making it obvious that he was ignoring her. Rachel laughed a little to herself. *How childish. As if I'm going to be sad that he isn't waving and smiling to me like he used to.*

She was just a few steps away from the car when she realized what the lyrics to the song were. An artist Rachel wasn't familiar with was singing, "My baby's come back home." After taking a moment to see if she recognized the voice, she shook her head, she didn't care who was singing. It didn't matter. What did matter though was the fact that Frank was trying to send her a message. But it was a message she was refusing to get. With head held high, she continued cleaning out her car without another glance in his direction. With the conference over, she was tired and ready to relax with a favorite movie. Stifling a yawn, she decided it would be a good idea to catch up on her sleep by going to bed early. Let Frank do what he wanted, she was going to have a good evening.

Mid-morning the next day, Rachel had some calls to make concerning the Valentine's Day Party she was planning for the youth and needed to stop by her office to get the phone numbers she needed.

She wasn't paying a lot of attention as she walked up to the car. But when she went to open the door, all other thoughts vanished when her eyes landed on a note taped to the window. She immediately recognized the writing. *Leave me alone, Frank!*

Annoyed, she pulled the tape off the glass and stuffed the envelope into her purse. She was pretty sure she was being watched and she was not about to give him the satisfaction of seeing her read it.

◦ ◦ ● ◉ ● ◦ ◦

Frank was standing by the window, beer in hand, watching as Rachel found his letter. When he realized she wasn't going to read it right then, he cursed. He may have been drunk when he had written it, but he knew it was a good letter. He'd said all the right things and he was certain that once she read it, his plan would be back on track. She would be coming back to his house, asking him to be friends again.

There was nothing to do now but wait. Sitting down in his recliner, he turned the TV on and opened another beer. At first he was angry when his boss fired him for being drunk at work. But now he was glad, he could sit and watch for her without worrying about missing anything. Things were turning out good after all.

· ◦ ● ● ◦ ·

When Rachel returned home from the office, she decided it was time to read the letter. Sitting on the couch with Shadow snuggled up on her lap, she pulled the paper out of the envelope. With just a glance, she could tell that he wasn't at his best when he wrote it. *I wonder if he drinks… or maybe does drugs?*

> "Hay RAchLe,
>
> I ThiNK I NO What you WaNT. ~~THes~~ PLase Tell ME your THougHTs ans FeeLing I'M SaRRy ~~I pushed~~ ThaT I MADe you MAd. NoW I Now Whate you wante.

I ~~would~~ WooD Still Like To geT To ~~KNOW~~ you. We can Still HavE good TiMes getting to NoiNg each outheR. DO NOT Hate me. We aRe Still friends RiGHT. I Care For You STILL. If you Need Me I BE THerE. Sow pLease DON'T Be UpSeT. ThiNgs will be a LoT BeTTeR Now you will see.

Frank.

P'S I ~~woul~~ wood Like To TaLK To you ALonE."

Rachel wasn't sure how long she sat there, staring at the disturbing words. The more she thought about it, the larger the knot in her stomach grew.

Shadow must have picked up on her emotions because the fuzzy dog stood up and stuck his head between Rachel and the note. With a silly little bark, he looked at her as if he were asking her what was wrong. Absentmindedly, she patted his head while she tried to make sense of it all.

"Oh, Shadow, what am I going to do? I'm a little scared." The dog turned his head and poked her arm with his wet nose. When Rachel had called her dad from the hotel, she had been angry. Speaking disrespectfully to her father was rarely something Rachel did, and though she regretted the way she had talked to him, she didn't regret telling him what had been happening. She had been reluctant to share with her parents just how troubled she felt because she was afraid they wouldn't take her seriously. And while she wasn't completely convinced her father fully grasped what was going on, it brought her relief to stop trying to keep the thing a secret. She was angry how the situation made her embarrassed, she felt as if she'd done something to deserve being treated the way Frank was treating her.

Rachel wasn't sure what she had expected her dad to do, but she had certainly thought he would do more than tell her to be cautious around Frank. That was it. A simple word of advice she had already given herself.

• ∘ ◦ ● ◦ ∘ •

The next time Rachel was outside, Frank came over.

"Hi, did you get my note?" he asked as she carried a bag of garbage to the trash can.

"Yes."

"So are things okay? How about we go get some coffee and we can talk about it. If I could just get you alone..." Rachel could see he was desperate to spend time with her. And that annoyed her. When would he understand that she didn't want to be around him?

"No Frank, I'm not going anywhere with you. I don't trust you and I don't like you. If you respected me at all, you would do as I asked. Leave me alone."

"You sure are a strong woman," Frank said with a smile. "I really like that about you."

"Frank, I'm more than strong, I'm stubborn. You might as well just give up; I'm not changing my mind."

"But..."

"Go away Frank!" Rachel shouted at him. *This is ridiculous; can I not even take out the trash without being bothered?*

Rachel stormed into the house and slammed the door. But the action only temporarily helped and over the next few days, every time she went outside, Frank was there. Not knowing what else to do, she decided to just ignore him. If she could get past her frustration, it was almost humorous. She would be doing whatever she needed to do, and he would be standing there talking to her as if she were listening. It was difficult at times, but she always managed to act as if she didn't even see him. After the third time this happened, she began to wonder when he would give up. Maybe he was just as stubborn as she was.

* ● ◦ ● ◦ ● ◦ ● ◦ ● ◦ ●

Rachel woke up screaming. She had dreamt he was chasing her, yelling, "If I could just get you alone!" And like all bad dreams go, she had tripped, giving him the chance to catch up to her. He was standing over her and she started screaming. It was the scream that woke her up.

Looking around, she assured herself she was safe at home and there was no danger. Peeking out the window, she saw that everything was quiet outside. She was finally starting to calm down when it dawned on her that her subconscious knew something important. The past few days when she had been ignoring Frank, she'd missed what he'd been saying. Her dream reminded her of what she'd heard him say over and over. Every time he talked to her he said, "If I could just get you alone," she just hadn't paid any attention to it... until now.

All the possibilities of what that could mean hit her like the winds of a hurricane. Every last shred of hope that he would give up was blown away and she went cold with fear. She refused, however, to give in to that fear and insisted that what she was feeling was wrong. *I'm letting my imagination get away from me. I'm fine. There's nothing to worry about. That prayer isn't being answered...*

Chapter 12

Rachel had been home alone for only a few minutes, but already she was feeling a little anxious. Her parents had taken a day trip up to Santa Rosa, California where her dad was speaking at a special event and Rachel was wondering if maybe she should have gone with them. Normally, Rachel enjoyed the peace and quiet of an empty house but lately, she couldn't get thoughts of Frank out of her mind.

She had stopped sharing her concerns with her parents because they assured her there wasn't anything to be overly concerned about. Plus, if she pressed the issue, she would have to tell them what she prayed when Violet was missing. And for some reason, she felt as if it wasn't something she should tell. Just saying it out loud could be the last action needed to set everything in motion. She was just going to be extra careful and stay away from Frank as much as she could and hope for the best.

While Rachel was deep in thought, the phone rang. She was hoping Violet would be available to hang out today and ran to the phone. *Maybe she got my message and is calling me back.* Since Violet started her online college classes, she hadn't had as much free time as she used to and Rachel was missing her friend.

"Hello! Riley Residence, this is Rachel," she answered with a cheerful voice.

"I was hoping you would answer the phone," Frank said.

Recognizing the voice, Rachel sighed in frustration. "Look, I thought I've made it clear to you that I have no interest in talking to you." Her voice was irritated.

"Oh, I know all about you and the little games you play," Frank said in a teasing voice.

"What in the world is that supposed to mean?"

"It means that I know what type of a girl you are. You've got everyone fooled, they think you're this innocent little thing, but I know you're not."

"Frank Smith! You are out of your mind!" Rachel was shaking now. Was it from fear? Or was it anger?

"You could just sneak out your window tonight and have a good time with me. We could... "

Rachel interrupted him as her shock escaped her lips. "What? You're Crazy!"

"I know you want to," Frank said in a soothing voice as if coaxing a small child. "I've seen the way you look at me."

"You're disgusting! I would never do such a thing! The only way I've looked at you is with disdain!"

"It's ok, baby. I promise I won't tell anyone."

Hearing Frank call her "baby" turned her stomach. She wanted to hang up, but she wasn't able to move. She was frozen, she couldn't make him stop talking and she couldn't make herself stop listening. So she just stood there with the phone to her ear, hearing the bizarre things he was saying.

"You can keep your parents in the dark, they don't have to know. And Violet, you don't have to tell her, either. It can be our secret."

"Leave me alone!" she yelled and threw the phone across the room. Her feet were moving before she had the sense to stop. They took her straight to the window and without really knowing why; she looked out at Frank's house. Sure enough, he was standing in his doorway. He held the phone in one hand and had a devious smile on his face. When he saw her, he raised his empty hand, pointed at her and winked.

• ◦ ◦ ● ◦ • •

The whole time Rachel was driving to Violet's house, she looked for him. There was no way she was going to lead him there. She would drive in circles for hours if that's what it took, but she was going to keep the location of Violet's house a secret.

She was certain he wasn't following her and that gave her a sense of peace. Now all she could do is hope that Violet was home.

When Rachel pulled into the driveway of the Thompson's home, she was relieved to see their van parked in front of the garage. *At least Cora's home; Violet probably is too, then.*

After parking her car, Rachel ran up the steps and rang the doorbell. Then she knocked. It felt like forever before the door opened. When Rachel saw Cora, she started crying.

"Frank scared me and I didn't know what to do!" Tears streamed down her face and she wiped them with a shaking hand. "Can I stay here?"

Cora wrapped her arms around Rachel and pulled her into the warm house.

"Of course you can, honey. Tell me all about it and we'll see what needs to be done."

* ◦ ◉ ◉ ◉ ◦ *

Frank missed her. How could that have happened? He had been looking out the window ever since he called her. He'd only stepped away once and that wasn't for long. Grabbing a beer from the refrigerator shouldn't have been long enough for her to drive away without him seeing her.

Oh well, it's not like I was going to go talk to her or anything. I already gave her enough to think about. She's probably making plans to come visit me tonight. I just need to be patient...

* ◦ ◉ ◉ ◉ ◦ *

"Rachel, I know I haven't talked about what happened in Mexico. And I really don't want to get into all that right now. It's just that some of the things he's saying remind me of... " Violet looked at her mom and started to cry. Cora reached out and put her hand on Violet's shoulder. "I'm sorry, I can't do this..." There were several minutes of silence before Violet cleared her throat and continued. "Just promise me you'll tell your parents that he scares you."

"Oh Violet, I'm sorry. I wish I could take the memories away for you." Rachel was more concerned about her friend than herself right now and missed the gravity of what Violet was saying.

"Rachel! Listen to me. This is about you right now, you need to get help. You can't handle this one on your own. I know you like being strong and independent, but this is a battle you can't fight by yourself."

"Violet's right, Rachel, you need to get help." Cora reached out and took Rachel's hand in her free one, the three were now connected. "And it's time to start praying."

After spending an hour in prayer, Rachel stayed in the safety of the Thompsons' house until late that night. But eventually, it was time to go home and talk to her parents. With a heavy heart and a tingle of fear, Rachel drove the short distance home. The night was heavy with fog and it added an eerie feeling to the darkness.

Thankful for the streetlight that illuminated her driveway she parked her car and got out. She had taken only two steps away from the car when she heard footsteps behind her. With a gasp, she turned and saw Frank just a few feet away. The smell of alcohol was heavy and it was easy to see that he was drunk. His eyes were glazed over, his shirt was stained and rumpled, and he was unsteady.

"There you are! I've been waiting for you. I thought we had a date!" He slurred the words out.

There was nothing to do but run. She didn't trust him when he was sober and she definitely wasn't going to trust him when he was drunk. Taking the steps two at a time, she hurried up the porch. But just like the dream she'd had the other day, she tripped. The toe of her shoe caught on the very last step and she went sprawling into the screen door. She tried to stop herself from falling, but wasn't fast enough. Her head hit the door first, and then her hands. She was so panicked; she didn't even feel the impact. All she could think about was getting inside.

As she was flung the screen door open, her dad opened the front door and pulled her in.

"Rachel! What's going on? Are you okay?" Dan asked as he looked at the blood dripping from a scratch on her forehead.

"No Dad, I'm not! It's been a horrible day!" Rachel flung herself into her father's arms and wept. Between sobs and hiccups, Rachel began telling her dad everything. From the information he already knew to the little details she had thought were unimportant. The only thing that remained a secret was the very thing she should have shared — her prayer.

Chapter 13

Frank had a terrible hang-over. His head was splitting and his stomach was still churning. It had been a few months since he'd been as drunk as he was last night and he guessed the time off had made his tolerance lower.

He could only remember a little of the day before. But what he did remember filled him with excitement. He had talked to Rachel and from what he could recall, she wanted to be with him. She'd said something about sneaking out at night, but that it needed to be a secret.

He was frantically gathering beer cans and trying to clean up the place. Phil had been away on business last night and was supposed to come home sometime today. If he did a good job, Phil would never know about his drinking binge. He didn't want to have to explain it to him. It would be the same conversation they'd had more times than he could count. Phil would tell him to get help and he would tell Phil to mind his own business.

Looking around, Frank was satisfied with his cleaning job. *There's only one thing left to do. I've got to get those cans out of here.*

Frank quickly tied up the bag full of cans, grabbed his keys, and walked to the door. He would need to take them to the recycling place; it wouldn't do to have Phil see them in the trash can. Frank was just a few steps away from his truck when he saw Dan and Mary walking across the street towards him.

"Mr. Riley! What can I do for you today?" Frank was all smiles.

"You can leave my daughter alone!" Dan said with anger. "I'll not have you scaring her any more. She doesn't want you hanging around her."

Frank was shocked, just for a minute. Then he remembered that Rachel wanted to keep their relationship a secret. It made sense, the overly protective father being fooled by a sneaky daughter. Rachel was smart, and strong, and stubborn. She knew what she was doing. Her parents thought she was innocent. But he knew different. He also knew how to play her little game.

"Yes sir! I'm sorry I've caused concern. You won't have any more problems."

It was as simple as that. Dan was satisfied and Mary, who hadn't said anything, appeared to be satisfied as well. *Okay, Rachel, two can play this game... and another game that's a lot more fun!*

◦ ∘●◉●∘ ◦

Rachel didn't come to him. He'd waited all day and night. But she never came. He was tired of waiting. He had to see her! But when he talked to them the other day, he'd told Dan and Mary that he wouldn't bother her.

Pacing the house, he thought and thought. He was on his third lap when it hit him. The Rileys thought they were related! He was halfway to their house when he had the plan completely figured out. And as he was knocking on their door, he was rehearsing what he was going to say.

"Hello, Mrs. Riley," Frank said when Mary answered the door. "I was just thinking this morning how much I miss my mom. I guess I'm just a bit homesick and I'm wondering if I might be able to hang out with my next of kin today."

"Oh, I guess..." Mary hesitated. Frank could tell she didn't know what to do. "I guess... "

Frank looked past Mary into the house; he could see Dan and Rachel were playing a game at the dinner table. There were glasses of milk and plates of cookies. It looked like they were having a great time, too. But the moment Rachel saw him, everything about her changed. *She's gone from laughing and happy, to frowning and angry. She's a good actress.*

"Why would you even talk to him?" Rachel said to Mary as she stormed up the stairs to her room. Dan, who had moved out of Rachel's way, walked up and stood next to his wife.

"Son, I think we really need to talk. I can't have you coming over here and making her upset."

"With all due respect, Mr. Riley, I'm not sure why she's upset." Frank was really trying. This had to go well; he needed them on his side. "Rachel and I might have started off on the wrong foot. I might have gotten the wrong impression about what she was wanting and all. But we talked it out and I just want to be part of the family. We're related. I want to know you guys and be able to call you friends. I'm hoping she can see that."

Dan looked Frank in the eye. "If what you're saying is the truth, you'll show it in your actions. When you start respecting her wishes, we just might believe you. And she wished to be left alone. Don't bother coming back here until things change."

As Dan closed the front door, Frank cursed. It hadn't gone as well as he'd planned.

· · · ● · · ·

The countdown to the start of the "Raise Them Up" Spring Tour had begun; only seven more days until the Rileys would spend five weeks speaking all over the state of California. These family focused mini-conferences would be held at various churches throughout the state and all three of the Rileys would be taking part. Mary would be teaching classes for people with babies and preschoolers. Dan would be working with those parenting children in grade school. And Rachel would, of course, be teaching parents of teenagers.

After Frank's failed attempt at fixing his relationship with the Rileys', he hadn't walked across the street to talk to Rachel. Nor had he called or left her any letters. Life would have been peaceful once again had it not been for his truck. While he was respecting Rachel's wishes, he was still making his presence known. Every day he would make laps around the block in his truck, and each time he drove in front of the Rileys' house, he revved the engine.

If that weren't enough, he seemed to always be in his front yard. It didn't matter what time of day. He was fixing a part on his truck, working in the garage or simply taking it easy in a lawn chair. While none of those things could be considered threatening, Rachel found them unnerving. He knew when she was home and when she wasn't. He watched her when she fed Shadow or took out the trash.

And since they were just one week from the tour, Rachel was making frequent trips from her house to the church. With each trip, he was watching her. Rachel was relieved that, unlike her father, she was to be gone the full five weeks. They had talked it over with the chairman of the deacons, and everyone had agreed that it was in Rachel's best interest not to come home for the weekends like she normally did. The women would stay at a hotel and Dan would come home and preach. There had also been a long discussion on how to maintain the safety of the church body and protect them from someone like Frank while still showing the love of Christ.

Maybe the time away would be enough to make Frank lose interest.

Chapter 14

The tour through California went fast and before she knew it, Rachel was home once again. The town's annual Fourth of July Parade and Festival was only two weeks away and Rachel was looking forward to the event. This year, her youth choir had been asked to sing before the fireworks began. Violet, who directed the choir, had chosen several patriotic songs and assigned solos to those she knew could sing them best. Since Rachel had been away when the practices began a few weeks ago, she wasn't participating like she normally did, but she was still able to join the practices and help where she was needed. Practices were being held every Tuesday and Thursday night for the next two weeks and Rachel planned to be at all of them.

"Mom, I have about an hour before choir. Was there anything you wanted me to do before I leave?" Rachel asked as she came into the kitchen where Mary was busy washing the dishes.

"You could make sure the laundry is going. The batch in the dryer might be done. I've been washing since we got home and I think I'm almost done!"

"Okay, I'll check on it." Rachel went into the laundry room and surveyed her mom's handiwork. There was a huge pile of clean laundry to be folded and just a few more loads to be washed. It was amazing how quickly her mom had gotten all that washed. They had only been home half a day!

After pulling the clothes out of the hot dryer, she took the wet clothing from the washing machine and put them in. Grabbing a dryer sheet, she tossed it in and started the machine. She quickly scooped up a load of jeans and put them in the washer, added soap and got them washing. She picked up a heaping basket of clothes and carried them into the living room to start the long process of folding.

It was almost time to go to church when she heard a huge crash outside. Wondering what happened, Rachel went to the window and looked out. She saw Phil and Frank in their front yard. They were obviously having an argument and it looked like Frank was winning. Phil's lankiness was no match for Frank's bulk. A few feet away from Phil, the trash can was lying on its side. It was dented and trash was strewn everywhere. *Did Frank throw the trash can at Phil?*

To Rachel's dismay, she watched as Frank picked up the recycling can, lifted it high into the air and threw it toward Phil. The can came down in another crash, just a few feet away from Phil. Rachel was well aware that Frank could have hit Phil if he wanted to. *At least he has a little self-control.*

"Frank! I'm warning you! If you don't get yourself under control, I'm kicking you out!" Phil yelled as he opened the front door and walked into the house. Frank started to follow him, and then stopped. He looked uncertain for just an instant, and started to glance around as if wondering who had seen the argument. When his eyes stopped at the window where Rachel stood, she gasped and stepped away. *Great, he knows I was watching him.*

• ◦ ●◉● ◦ •

Frank was angry. Who did Phil think he was? He had no right to tell him to leave Rachel alone. He'd gone five weeks without seeing her; it was impossible for him to stay away from her any longer.

But he was angry with himself because he should have been more careful. He didn't want Rachel to know he had an anger problem. That wouldn't help anything. *I've got to talk to her. Maybe I can explain things.*

Frank peeked out the window and saw that Rachel's car was in the driveway. The sooner he talked to her the better. He debated whether to call or walk across the street and talk in person. After thinking how nice it would be to see her smile, he decided to walk over.

When Frank knocked on the door, he assumed Rachel would be the one to answer and was surprised when Mary was there instead.

"Hi, Mary! It's good to have my family back home!" Frank said with a charming smile. "Is Rachel around? There's something I wanted to talk to her about."

"Frank, she's not here and even if she was, you know she doesn't want to talk to you." Mary's firmness surprised him. She started to close the door, but he reached out his foot and placed it between the door and threshold, keeping it open.

"I'm not too sure I believe you. Her car's sitting right there. I think you're trying to keep us apart." There was a glint of anger in his eye.

"You can think all you want, but she's at the church. Now, if you'll please leave, I have some things to attend to." When Frank moved his foot, Mary firmly shut the door and left him standing there holding the screen door open.

"You can't boss her around forever you know!" Frank yelled through the door.

◦ ◦ ● ● ◦ ◦

Rachel and Dan had been at church about twenty minutes when Frank showed up. Rachel was up on the platform with Violet and the choir. Dan was sitting down at the soundboard. The sound man had called earlier saying he was sick and needed someone to fill in for him. Dan was planning on going to the church that night anyway, so he had agreed to get the choir started before he went to his office to finish his sermon.

The moment she saw him, Rachel panicked. *How did he know I was here? I rode with Dad so he wouldn't know where I went!*

Excusing herself, Rachel quickly walked down the aisle to the back of the sanctuary where her father sat.

"Frank's here!" Rachel said in the calmest voice she could manage. After seeing his display of anger, she was even more determined to avoid him. "You've got to do something. I don't want to talk to him!"

"Don't worry. I'll take care of it." And with that, Dan left the sanctuary and walked up to Frank.

Uncertain of what she should do, Rachel decided to return to her spot on the stage. From where she stood, she could see Frank and her father talking in the foyer. The glass windows at the back of the sanctuary gave the building a nice open feel, but Rachel was wishing the windows weren't there. She was also wishing she had remained down at the soundboard. Between the windows and her being up on stage, Frank had the ability to look at her. And the whole time Dan was talking to him, Frank was staring right at her.

After a few minutes of arguing with Dan, Frank finally left, and both Rachel and her father sighed in relief. But instead of going and finishing his sermon, Dan stayed in the sanctuary just in case Frank decided to come back.

When Dan and Rachel drove home later that night, he told her that Frank claimed she had asked him to watch the practice. Even though Dan didn't believe him, it still bothered her. Frank was lying about her now. And not everyone was going to know the truth of the situation like her parents did.

Then, when they returned home, Mary told them what had happened and it bothered Rachel greatly that Frank had yelled at her mom. Mary had been so troubled by her altercation with Frank that she had tried to call the church, but they had been so preoccupied with Frank themselves that they never even heard the phone ring. *What have I done to make him think I want to be with him? How many times do I have to tell him to leave me alone?*

The events of the day replayed in her mind and robbed her of sleep. It was late and she should be asleep by now. It seemed unreal that she had returned home just that morning. *I haven't been home twenty-four hours and he's already tried to talk to me twice!*

As she was pacing the floor, trying to make sense of things, she heard a bark outside. Wondering if it was Shadow, she went to her window and carefully pulled back the curtain. She didn't want Frank to see her if he was watching. When her eyes adjusted to the darkness outside, she saw Shadow walking across the street towards Frank's house. The ornery dog had gotten out of his fenced yard again! With a feeling of being betrayed, she watched as Frank held out a dish for Shadow. The dog greedily ate whatever Frank was offering him and when he was done, Shadow hopped up into Frank's lap. Frank sat there petting the black dog with a smile on his lips.

Anger welled up inside Rachel and she wanted to yell. Instead, she picked up a shoe and threw it at the wall. Was nothing sacred? How was it that Frank seemed to be involved in every part of her life?

A familiar tingle washed over her. Why did she always have to think about that prayer?

Chapter 15

Even though they were filled will annoying reminders that Frank lived across the street, the weeks until the Fourth of July went fast. As Rachel was getting ready for the parade and choir performance, she wondered if Frank was going to be there.

Looking in her closet, she picked out the most modest articles of clothing she could find. *I wouldn't want to give him any more reasons to like me.* After taking the clothes off the hanger, she walked over to her bed and set them down. She still had a few minutes before she needed to get ready. Deciding to read her Bible, she sat down on the floor, crossed her legs and picked up the green, leather bound book. Quickly thumbing through the pages, she stopped at a familiar passage. She actually quoted the words of Romans 8:38 and 39 before she read them. "For I am persuaded that neither death, nor life, nor angels, nor principalities, nor powers, nor things present, nor things yet to come, nor height, nor depth, nor any other created thing shall be able to separate us from the love of God which is in Christ Jesus our Lord."

Rachel had memorized the passage when she was just nine years old, and it still stirred her heart. She took time to savor the words on the page. *Nothing, not even Frank can separate me from God, and for that I am incredibly thankful!*

If Shadow hadn't walked in and started rubbing his face on her arms, she might have stayed there praying long after she was supposed to leave for the parade. Looking at the clock, Rachel realized she was late. She hurried and dressed in red, white and blue. Pulling her hair into a pony tail, she tied it off with a festive ribbon, then ran down the stairs in search of her shoes and purse.

"Bye, Mom! Bye, Dad! I'll see you there!" she called out as she ran out the door.

As Rachel backed out of her driveway, she looked in the rear view just in time to see Frank come out of his house and walk to his truck. *Where's he going?*

It didn't take long for Rachel to see that he was following her. For a brief minute, she thought about taking the back roads to see if he truly was following her. But she decided to act as if she was unaware of his presence. *He's following me and we both know it. If I drive different than I normally would, then he gets the satisfaction of knowing he can change the way I act.*

So whether it was the right thing to do or not, Rachel drove straight to the church where the choir's parade float was waiting. As she pulled into the church parking lot, Frank followed her. She was beginning to wonder what he planned to do. When she parked, he parked next to her. Then he looked over at her and grinned. It took a lot of self-control, but she managed to ignore him after that. As she gathered her purse and some things she needed for later, she saw him back out of the parking spot and drive away.

◦ ◦ ◉◉ ◦ ◦

Frank joined the crowd lining Main Street. The parade was to begin in ten minutes. He still had plenty of time to find the perfect spot. He wanted to be where she would see him and he looked for a place on a corner. The path the parade was to take wasn't very long; it was a small town, after all. So his choices were limited. Finally deciding on a spot near the park where the other festivities were to take place, he sat down and waited for the parade to start.

After watching the school's marching band and the fire trucks, he saw the first float. It seemed like every business and church in the town had entered a float, but he didn't notice much about any of them. All he cared about was the one Rachel was on. And when he spotted it, time seemed to stand still. The float was decorated in red, white and blue streamers. The youth choir was seated and singing "God Bless America" while Violet directed them. And much like the other floats, Frank hardly noticed those details. His eyes were riveted on the person standing in the middle of the float. Rachel was dressed up like the Statue of Liberty. And she looked almost regal. With a paper torch in one hand, books in the other, she smiled at the crowd.

His heart caught a little as the float neared the spot where he sat. In a second, she would see him. And when she did, he just knew she would be thrilled that he was there. He was so excited his fingers tingled and his breath came in short gasps. Then, the moment he'd been waiting for arrived. With a beautiful smile and eyes that were filled with merriment, she looked at him. But what happened next left him short of breath for a whole different reason than he had hoped for. When she had seen him, her smile faded and her eyes went dark. *Why does she look at me like that? I've got to talk to her!*

• • ● • •

For the rest of the day, Frank followed Rachel wherever she went. The fact that he never approached her gave her the feeling that he wanted to talk to her but was waiting until she was alone. As she stood in line to get her favorite carnival food, she said a small, grateful prayer that Violet's presence seemed to keep Frank away.

The line started moving and Rachel took a step forward. She was looking around for Violet, hoping to find her soon. The girls had disagreed on what to eat, so they had separated just long enough to purchase their food. As she was searching for her friend, the line moved once again and she absentmindedly took a step forward to close the gap. She was taken by surprise when she bumped into someone. The impact knocked her off balance and she would have fallen if the stranger hadn't reached out and took her arm. With embarrassment, she looked up and apologized.

"I'm so sorry! Thank... Oh, Phil, it's you!" Rachel started laughing when she realized she had just run into her neighbor.

"Are you ok?" Phil responded as he let go of her arm.

"I am. Thank you." Rachel hesitated before asking the question that was burning inside her. "Phil, what's up with your brother? Why won't he just leave me alone?"

The questions made Phil visibly uncomfortable and Rachel wondered for a moment if she had made a mistake in asking him.

"Well, I suppose he's just acting how all men act when they're infatuated with a pretty girl." Phil refused to look at her.

"But, our grandmothers may have only been friends, but from what I've been told, they treated each other as sisters. He doesn't see anything wrong with that?" Rachel just wasn't satisfied with Phil's answer.

Phil turned and looked at her now. With a curse of frustration, he shook his head.

"I promised not to tell. But, shoot! Our families never knew each other. He lied."

"He lied? But... but... why? I don't..." Rachel had a hard time expressing all the things swirling around in her head.

Phil acted upset and even more uncomfortable than he had before. He stood there looking at her as if he was unsure what to do next. Then, before she was able to ask any more questions, he ran off.

Chapter 16

"I just can't believe he doesn't have a family connection after all," Violet said as Rachel backed out of the Thompsons' driveway.

"Honestly, I have to say I'm not all that surprised," Rachel said. "It makes sense."

"So now you've got this random guy who's infatuated with you. Kind of makes you want to go back and not go to that movie with him, huh? I'm sorry I wasn't able to go. But you should have canceled, you didn't have to go."

"You're telling me! Life feels so crazy right now." Rachel shook her head in frustration. Just thinking about Frank made her stomach turn.

"Whoa, Rach, you're gripping the steering wheel so hard your knuckles are turning white!" Violet looked at her friend with concern.

"It's just that he makes me so angry... and scared." Rachel didn't say anything for a few minutes. Then suddenly, she realized what Violet had said. "Wait. What did you call me?"

"I called you Rach. I think it's high time I found a nickname for you. Don't you think?" Violet grinned at her friend and batted her brown eyes.

"Whatever, Vi." Rachel giggled.

As Rachel made the turn onto Highway 1, she looked in her rear view mirror. What she saw filled her with dread. She wished for just a split second that she was a cursing girl, she could think of a lot of words she's like to use right then.

"Vi, it looks like we have company," Rachel said through clenched teeth. Violet turned to look behind them. "Oh, my word! He just waved at me! Rachel, this guy is crazy!"

"What should we do? We can't just go to the beach if Frank is following us!" Rachel said in a panicked voice.

"Well, we don't know for sure that he's following us. And right now, since there are still a few turnoffs, he doesn't know if we're going to Fort Bragg or to the Botanical Gardens or to the beach. Although, since it's raining, I would imagine he thinks we're going to Fort Bragg," Violet said logically. "Let's drive for a few more miles and see what happens."

"Okay, that sounds good."

Rachel drove on for a few more miles and Frank stayed right behind them. Every turn she passed, he passed. She was now heading towards Fort Bragg, even though they were originally going to the beach.

"Violet, this is ridiculous. What should we do? I don't know what we should do!"

"We should go home. Let's turn around at the next road. I think its Garden View Road coming up. It's real wide, you'll be able to just pull off the road and loop around to get back on the highway and go home."

"Good thinking. It does that 'Y' thing with all the gravel in the middle. That will be perfect." Rachel started to feel calmer once the plan was decided on. She was grateful Violet was with her; sometimes Frank scared her so much she didn't know what to do. *Darn it Frank, I hate how you can make me feel so helpless. I feel like a deer caught in the headlights, and I'm bracing myself for when you hurt me...*

"Rachel, there's the turnoff, you better slow down or you'll miss it." Violet broke into Rachel's thoughts, once again making her grateful for her clear headed thinking.

Rachel stepped on the brake and made a right hand turn onto Garden View Road. Once they were on the road, she made a U-turn and pulled back up to Highway 1. Just like she thought he would, Frank turned off, too. But instead of looping around, he simply drove his truck right up to her car. She was sitting at the stop sign, waiting for a break in traffic so she could pull out onto the highway, and the hood of his truck was pointed directly at the side of her car.

"What's he doing?" Rachel yelled at Violet.

"I don't know... " Violet said as she locked her door. "Quick, Rachel! Lock your door!"

"Violet! He's getting out of his truck! What do I do! I can't go yet, there's a long line of cars!" Rachel looked at Violet, then back at the rain drenched road. Once again she was gripping the steering wheel too hard, turning her knuckles white.

Frank walked up to her window and motioned for her to roll it down.

"Come on, Rachel! I need to talk to you!" He was yelling while he shielded his face from the wind and rain.

"Don't look at him, Rachel. Just ignore him!" Violet encouraged Rachel. "Okay, I think there's your chance. See it? You can go right after that blue car."

Rachel thought her heart was going to explode. She had Frank on one side of her yelling at her to talk to him. Violet was on the other side telling her what to do. And there were a bunch of cars going sixty miles an hour on a wet, slippery road in front of her.

"Go, Rachel! Now! Just floor it!" Violet was screaming.

Without thinking, Rachel pushed the accelerator to the floor. Gravel and mud flew up and showered down on Frank as she sped away. Violet looked behind them and started to laugh.

"I think you showed him! He's flapping his arms and yelling."

"Violet, what do we do now?" Rachel asked.

"Well, I think you should go home. I can either stay with you or have my mom pick me up."

"Yeah, it might be nice to have you there when I tell my parents what happened just now."

The girls drove in silence for a while, each lost in their own thoughts. Then all of a sudden, Frank's truck appeared out of nowhere. The girls both screamed as he pulled up behind them, honking his horn and waving his arm out the window. When there was a passing lane, he sped up and drove alongside them. He was so focused on yelling at Rachel, he started swerving.

"You've got to lose him. Do you think you can go faster than him?"

"Are you kidding me? This is a hot rod; of course my car goes faster. But Vi, that will get us killed! These roads are slick."

"Just go faster and pray! He's going to side swipe you if you don't do something!"

Rachel pushed the gas pedal all the way down and drove like a madwoman while Violet prayed out loud for God to intervene. Frank tailed them all the way back into town. But as they were entering Casper, Rachel was able to go through a yellow light leaving Frank caught in the red light.

"Thank you, Lord! It's a miracle he didn't run the light!"

"He probably saw the police car sitting at the intersection." Violet sighed then turned to look at Rachel. "We can't go to your house. He knows a million different ways to get there. He could get there before we do. He could be waiting for us. Do you know for sure that your parents are home?"

"No, I don't know for sure. What should we do?"

"Let's go to my house. I know both my mom and dad are home."

It only took a few minutes for Rachel to navigate the streets that took them to the Thompson residence. Both girls were certain Frank had stopped following them and with a prayer of thanks they pulled into Violet's driveway.

"We made it!" Violet smiled at Rachel.

"Yes, we did." *Now I just have to figure out what to do next.*

Chapter 17

Frank woke to someone pounding on his front door. Knowing that Phil had left for work hours earlier, Frank forced his body out of bed. If he thought the person would just go away, he would have stayed in bed. But the knocking was insistent; whoever they were, they weren't going to leave anytime soon.

As he walked to the door, he ran a hand through his hair. *I must look a mess. I hope it isn't Rachel.* When Frank opened the door, he was shocked. There stood Dan Riley, and he wasn't happy.

"Mr. Riley. Good morning." Frank tried to be charming.

"There's nothing good about this morning and you know it! How dare you scare my daughter like that! Who do you think you are anyway? First you lie to us and now you won't leave her alone!"

"Well, I... I... " Frank couldn't think of anything to say.

"You will never do that again! Do you understand?"

"No sir, I don't understand. What are you talking about?"

"What am I talking about? My daughter was in tears when I got home last night. She said you followed her out of town and you were yelling at her."

"Mr. Riley, Sir, I'm sorry." Frank honestly was sorry. "I was only trying to talk to her. You know how girls are, she's overreacting. I swear I wasn't yelling and I truly didn't mean to scare her."

"I don't care what you were *meaning* to do. I'm telling you what you did! And you will not do it again. I promise you, if you do it again, you'll regret it."

Dan was barely controlling his anger and Frank could tell. He would have loved a fight with Dan, but he knew it was in his best interest to just let Dan have his say. He knew Violet, Dan, and Mary were all trying to keep Rachel away from him and he certainly didn't want to give them more reasons to keep trying. The sooner they gave up, the better. And if they didn't give up, well, things were still going to go the way he wanted. It was just going to take more time and effort.

After Dan stormed off, Frank sat close to the window the rest of the day. Dan may have tried to scare him away from Rachel, but that wasn't going to work. The next time he saw Rachel drive away, he was going to follow her and ask if she knew her dad was trying to keep them apart. Frank knew she was loyal, but he was pretty sure that once she heard what was going on, she would decide to stop listening to them. She was an adult after all, and it was time for her to shake off her parent's restrictions and have a little fun.

Just when Frank was about to give up, Rachel walked out of her house. He noticed she had her purse and it looked like she was going somewhere. He quickly jumped off the couch and put his shoes on. As soon as she drove away, he would get in his truck and follow.

Standing close to the window again, he groaned as he watched her pick up Shadow. He'd been waiting for hours, and now that she was finally going somewhere, she was wasting time on that stupid dog! *Just get in the car, Rachel!*

⸰ ⸰ ◦◉◦ ⸰ ⸰

The day had been a long one for Rachel. After what happened the night before, she hadn't slept well. Then, when her dad came back from talking to Frank, they had sat and discussed the situation for several hours. It was a long, exhausting conversation that had only made Rachel more confused and unsettled.

What she needed was chocolate. Maybe some ice cream, or cookies. So without a second thought, she said goodbye to her parents and went to buy a treat to brighten her day. After snuggling with Shadow for a few minutes, she got into the car and drove to the larger of the two grocery stores in Casper.

She was standing in the cookie aisle when he found her. She had chocolate ice cream and a jar of hot fudge sauce already in the cart and was reaching for a box of fudge covered cookies when the sound of her name caused her to jump. Her breath caught when she saw who had startled her.

"Frank!" she whispered.

"Did you know your dad visited me this morning?"

"Yes, I did. And I agree with everything he told you." She barely kept her voice from wavering. "I don't want to see you again. I want you to leave me alone."

"Rachel, honey, you don't need to pretend. I know you want to please your parents... " Frank looked sincere. And his eyes even held gentleness. "But I know you'd rather be pleasing me."

"What in the world? I don't think I heard you right!" Rachel was angry now.

The nerve of this guy! He thinks he knows me! All he knows is I'm a strong woman... well, he hasn't seen anything yet. I'm stronger than he realizes...

"You can please me real easy." Rachel looked at him coyly. Taking a step closer to him, she looked right into his dark brown eyes. She smiled a little, and then quickly changed from coy to defiant. "All you have to do is leave me alone. I never want to see you again!"

Rachel turned and started to leave, but Frank grabbed the shopping cart and stopped her.

"I admire your strength, Rachel. It's one of the things I like most about you. But I'm stronger. Just you wait; you'll be seeing things my way soon enough. I guarantee it."

Frank let go of the cart and walked away. Rachel wasn't certain how long she stood there, but when someone asked if she needed help, she realized her ice cream was starting to melt.

"No, I'm ah... I'm fine." She said more to herself than the woman looking at her with concern. She should have let her mom come with her, but when Mary had suggested it, Rachel had assured her she would be okay. She had simply gone to the grocery store; there should have been no harm in that. *I guess I can't be alone anymore.*

With a smile she knew wasn't convincing, Rachel held the eyes of the lady, "I'll be just fine."

Chapter 18

"Wow, Violet, that was so not funny!" Rachel said as they walked out of the restaurant.

"It was to me! You should have seen the look on your face when I told the waiter it was your birthday." Violet was still laughing.

"But you lied!" Rachel pretended to glare at Violet. "My birthday isn't for a whole week. You just wanted to see me wear that stupid sombrero they make people put on when it's their birthday."

"Oh snap! I should have gotten a picture. The youth would have loved seeing it."

Rachel poked Violet in the ribs. "You're horrible, you know that?" "But you love me."

"That I do. I don't know what I would do through this whole Frank mess if it wasn't for you making me laugh and forget about him from time to time. It's hard to believe it's almost August already and he's still bothering me. This lunch has been a great break from reality."

"You're more than welcome. Believe me; this will pass, Rach. Tough times don't last forever."

The girls reached the car and got in. Rachel hadn't wanted to drive today since she had such an easy car to spot, but Violet's car had been in the shop, so they didn't have much choice. To stay on the safe side, they had decided to stay in their home town and not venture out to Fort Bragg. That way if something happened, they would be closer to home.

Rachel dropped Violet off at her home and was making the short trip back to her own house when it happened. Frank showed up. They were going opposite directions on a residential street. He passed her without even looking her way and Rachel sighed in relief. Maybe he was finally going to leave her alone. But just a few blocks later, as she was waiting at a four way stop, he appeared again. This time he looked at her, and then turned onto a side street. *Okay, what game are you playing? Are you going to go around the block and come back again?*

Sure enough, that's just what he did. Frank pulled his big truck onto the road a few blocks in front of Rachel, and was driving towards her. Then, as he neared her car, he pulled into her lane and accelerated. She watched in horror as his truck lurched forward at the sudden increase in speed.

"What are you doing?" Rachel yelled as if he could hear her. "What are you doing?"

Rachel knew she only had a split second to decide what to do. Looking to her right, she saw she couldn't pull to the side of the road because there were cars parked along the curb. She had nowhere to go.

Knowing she was at his mercy, she slammed on the brakes and hoped for the best. As Frank's truck came speeding closer, she braced herself for the impact and screamed. "Please don't do this!"

Frank's bumper was inches away from the hood of her car after he stomped on the brakes. With smoking tires, he backed up and then pulled the truck into his lane. He slowly crept forward until he was side by side with her. Rolling down his window, he turned and stared at her. The expression on his face held a warning and a promise. This wasn't the end. With a smile that communicated a challenge, he drove away.

If it hadn't been for the adrenaline pumping through her veins, she would never have been able to drive the six blocks home. When she pulled into her driveway, the tears started to fall and by the time she got into the house, she was sobbing.

* ◦ ◉◍◉ ◦ ◦

"That's it! I'm calling the police. This has gone way too far." Dan stormed to get the phone. "I'm just glad I decided to study at home today and was here when you came home. This can't wait and I'm putting a stop to it right now."

Mary was trying to calm Rachel down and wondered if she needed to try and calm Dan down, too.

"Mom, I was so scared. I thought for sure he was going to hit me!" Rachel was still shivering. Though she wasn't crying anymore, every now and then her breath would catch in a weird hiccup.

"Hello! Yes, I need an officer to come out right away," Dan said when the police station's operator answered the phone. "Yes, that's right. 7091 Ocean Heights Drive... yes, okay... thank you."

"Are they coming?" Mary asked.

"They said it would be about twenty minutes."

"All right, Rachel, Sweetie, let's make some tea." Mary led Rachel to the dining table and got her comfortable. Then she went into the kitchen and set the teapot on the stove. "Some tea will help you relax."

"I doubt I can relax with the police here, Mom," Rachel said as she rubbed her temples. *When will this be over?*

As the three of them gathered at the table with mugs of tea warming their hands, Dan looked at Rachel with tears in his eyes. "Sweetheart, I'm so very sorry I didn't listen to you the very first time you questioned the way Frank made you feel." Rachel couldn't respond, all she could do was nod her head to acknowledge the apology.

"Oh baby, I was so naïve." Mary almost spilled her tea as she reached out to hug her daughter. "I never even thought something like this would ever happen to you."

After waiting for twenty-five minutes, the doorbell finally rang and Dan ran to open the door.

"Come in, I'm Dan Riley." Dan stepped aside and let the red haired policeman through the door. "This is my wife,

Mary, and my daughter, Rachel." Dan pointed to the women sitting at the dining room table and urged the officer to sit.

"Nice to meet you all; my name is Officer Shawn Sinclair," Shawn said as he joined the women at the table. "So what seems to be the trouble?"

"Well, my neighbor won't leave me alone. And now, he just tried to run me off the road or something." Rachel began telling the officer the whole story.

When she had finished telling him all the events since Frank had moved to Casper, Shawn asked if she had kept the letters.

"Actually, I did. Let me go get them," Rachel said as she rose from where she was sitting and started up the stairs.

While she was gone, Shawn asked Dan and Mary more questions and by the time Rachel returned, there wasn't much more to do than get the paper work started.

"Here, Rachel, you can start filling these out while I take a look at the letters." Shawn said as he handed her a stack of forms.

While Rachel worked her way through the papers, Shawn thoroughly looked at the words written by Frank's hand. Every now and then Shawn would shake his head. He read them again before placing them in an envelope to turn in as evidence.

"I have to say, these letters bear the mark of a stalker. I've seen it many times. I worked in Los Angeles before I moved here and I saw a lot of these cases."

"Wh… what makes you so certain he's a stalker?" Rachel asked, knowing her worst fears were being confirmed.

"Well, see how he's mixed up all the upper and lower case letters? Then, look at this one here." Shawn held out the note that had been taped to her car window. "See how he wrote and crossed out so many things? That shows he wasn't thinking clearly when he wrote it. It shows irrational behavior. Some of the phrases he uses are classic as well."

Mary was growing paler by the moment. "Lord, protect our daughter!" Mary prayed out loud.

Shawn looked at Rachel for a moment as if evaluating her and then he said something curious. "All this makes sense. He fits the typical markings of a stalker, and you fit the typical markings of someone being stalked."

"I'm sorry, what are you saying?" Dan asked, not certain he liked the man's comment.

"I'm saying that Miss Riley here fits the situation. She's well known; most people around here know your family. And some of us think of you as a kind of celebrity, what with your traveling and all. She's petite and looks vulnerable because of her size. Also, she's beautiful and has a personality you don't often see. All those things together, well, they make her a target."

"Officer Sinclair, I understand what you are saying. And I can't tell you it makes me feel good about the situation." Rachel looked at her parents, and then looked back to Shawn. "I have a concern and I'm wondering if you can help me resolve the problem?"

"What's that?"

"Well, as you know, I am the youth director at my dad's church. So every Wednesday night I lead a Bible study at the church. Do you think I will be putting my youth in danger by continuing to hold those meetings? It breaks my heart to think they might be affected by all this."

"Well, I think I can solve that problem easily," Shawn smiled. "I'm on a rotation schedule, but I have some Wednesday nights off. So on those nights, I'll just come on down to the church and help out. And on the nights I'm working, I'll make sure my rounds cover the church during that time. I'll check in on you and make sure everything's okay. And when I can't, I have some buddies who will. No need to be worried. I'll make it my personal goal to make sure Frank stays off church property."

"Okay, that sounds good," Dan said. "But I think we'll need to have a meeting with the parents as well. They might want to help, too. Or they may simply want to keep their kids at home for a while."

"Like I said, I'll make sure Frank leaves the youth alone." Shawn's jaw was set in determination. "Then I guess we're all set. You've filled out all the paperwork and I have it here. Is there anything else you can think of that I might need to know?"

Rachel watched as her parents looked thoughtful for a few minutes before confirming that everything was taken care of. Rachel on the other hand, did think of something, but couldn't bring herself to share it. *I'll just sound silly. And besides, why would a police officer care about a prayer?*

After bidding the Rileys a good night, Officer Sinclair left. As soon as Shawn was out the door, the Rileys stood in a circle and prayed. They prayed for Rachel's safety and for wisdom concerning the days ahead. They prayed the stalking order would be granted and the issue would be resolved soon. Then, like they always did, they turned their focus away from themselves and offered up a prayer for an unbeliever. They prayed for Frank.

Chapter 19

It had been a mistake. Even while he was circling the block, he had known it was a stupid thing to do. Scaring Rachel was something he had done in spite of his better judgment. He had felt a thrill when he saw her panic, and at the time, it felt good.

But when he saw the police car drive up and park in front of their house last night, the thrill was gone. Instead, he was filled with dread. He'd had a few run-ins with the law already and wasn't excited at the idea of going through that again.

Not knowing what to do, he had simply tried to ignore the guilt growing inside him. But it hadn't worked. After a whole day of unsuccessfully trying to forget his stupid choice, he went to the bar to drown his troubles. There was nothing like the sweet escape of alcohol. Too bad morning had to come and remind him of his actions. When he had awoken early this morning and looked out the window, Rachel's house was shrouded in fog. Frank wasn't normally the type to notice such things, but as he watched the white mist swirl around the little house, he thought it gave the home a look of sadness.

Filled with regret, Frank threw the curtain back in place and punched the wall. Shaking his hand, he stood there and stared at the hole left in the drywall. *I've got to get some air.*

Frank walked to the table and picked up his keys. He grabbed a jacket on his way out the door and got into his truck. Once he made his way out to Highway 1, he pushed the gas pedal to the floor. In a matter of moments, he'd reached a speed that was dangerous on the curvy highway. He was entering the last big curve before Fort Bragg when he passed a police car sitting on the side of the road. Seeing the black and white vehicle, Frank swore and stomped on the brake to slow down. Then, he quickly moved his foot to the other pedal and sped up. *Maybe I can outrun them.* When he heard the siren and saw the lights flashing behind him, he changed his mind and once again stepped on the brake. When he found a spot that was wide enough, he pulled the truck off the road and parked on the shoulder. He rummaged through the papers and garbage cluttering the passenger seat until he found his wallet. He pulled out his driver's license, and then opened the glove box to find his proof of registration and insurance. Hoping his cooperation would make things go better, he looked in the rearview mirror to watch the officer approach.

Before the policeman even neared the truck, Frank rolled down the window and held the papers out. Without a word, the officer walked up and took them. When he read the name on the documents, his face showed surprise.

"I'm Officer Sinclair, and you're Mr. Frank Smith," Shawn said with a serious glint in his eye. "That being said, it looks like your speeding this afternoon has saved me some time."

Frank looked at the stocky man and wondered where he'd seen him before. *There's something familiar about this guy. Was he the officer at Rachel's house?*

"I have something to give you. I was going to wait until you were home, but this seems like as good a time as any." Shawn held out an envelope. "It looks like you're getting issued a subpoena along with your speeding ticket. You also have a headlight out and according to my records, you've already been issued a fix it ticket. So now you'll be issued a fine. I'd say today isn't your lucky day, Mr. Smith."

Frank opened the envelope and read the letter. Shock registered on his face and he went pale.

"What... ah... what is this for?" he asked.

"It's all right there on that paper. You'll be notified when your arraignment is scheduled." Shawn said with a slight smile. "You just sit tight while I write those tickets up for you."

⋄ ⋄ ⦿ ⦿ ⦿ ⋄ ⋄

Rachel was locking up the church after a long day. The youth camping trip was quickly approaching and she still had a few registration forms to turn in. Plus, she needed to figure out the details of carpooling; that detail had become more difficult since Rachel was coordinating the trip with two other churches in the area. One of her dreams was of building a community of people reaching out to youth with one purpose and focus. Little by little, her goal was being accomplished and the local churches were starting to join together.

With tired steps, Rachel walked from the church to her car. Just as she was getting in, Officer Sinclair drove into the parking lot. Seeing him, she waited outside of the car and stood there while he parked.

"What's up, Shawn?" she asked with a cheerful smile. Officer Sinclair had proven to be a man of his word and had been faithfully watching out for her. It wasn't uncommon for her to see him drive by the church or her home. He hadn't come to youth group yet, but she already felt much safer knowing he was keeping an eye on her.

"I have something for you." He walked up to her and handed her a subpoena. "I'm sorry, but it looks like you're going to court. I don't know what the future has in store in regards to all this, but know that I'm on your side."

"Thank you. That means a lot."

"Is everything okay?" Shawn asked as he began to look around. "Has he been bothering you?"

"Nothing worse than his attempts to remind me he's still across the street," Rachel shrugged. "He's still trying to get my attention, but he's stayed on his side of the street and has behaved himself. It's only been a week, so I'm not holding my breath," Rachel sighed as she held up the envelope. "But I sure hope there's an end in sight."

"I hear you... I hear you," Shawn said as he started to walk back to his car. "I have to get going. Be careful."

When Shawn drove away, Rachel sat down in her car and opened the envelope.

"So I'm going to court," she said to herself. "I'll have to go before a judge... "

Differing emotions surged through Rachel as she stared at the subpoena in her hand. Part of her was relieved that an end was in sight, but the other part was terrified. *What if the judge doesn't like me? What if I don't get the protective stalking order?*

∘ ∘ ◉ ◉ ◉ ∘ ∘

"Sweetie, did you call that number?" Mary asked.

"Yes. I did." Rachel looked up from the paper sitting on the table. The phone was still clutched in her hand and her heart was beating fast. "Mom, it just seems so strange that I'm talking to the victims' advocate. I feel weird." Rachel slammed her hand down on the table in frustration. "I don't know why, but I feel like I've done something wrong."

Mary walked over and placed a hand on her daughter's shoulder. "Oh, honey. You've done nothing wrong. It's not your fault; Frank is the one that's weird."

"I know, Mom. But I still have this voice telling me I must have done something to make him think I'm interested in the things he's suggested. Do I dress inappropriately?"

Rachel shook her head even as the words were out. "You don't have to answer that, Mom. I know I don't. I guess I just doubt myself."

"Don't doubt, trust God to direct you like you've always done. But honey, I wanted to talk to you about some information I read today. Officer Sinclair stopped by with a pamphlet from the Women's Center. I read it and honestly I am shocked to learn that this kind of stuff happens all the time."

"Why, Mom, why doesn't the world wake up and put a stop to it?"

"Oh I don't know, maybe a lack of information? I was so naïve and trusting!"

Sighing, Rachel placed her arms on the table and rested her head on them. "I suppose all the secrecy on my part didn't help either. I know it doesn't apply, but I was embarrassed. But instead of letting the embarrassment cause me to hide reality, I should have seen it for the warning sign that it was."

"What do you say about making an appointment to meet with one of the Women's Center's counselors? We need to know what is happening in the world so we can not only prevent harm coming to you, but so we can help other women, too."

Rachel nodded in agreement.

"Just so you know, the arraignment is the Monday after I get back from camp. The lady I talked to told me the arraignment would tell us exactly what they are charging him with and why we are going to court."

"That worked out good. You can go to camp and have something else to think about while you're waiting," Mary said with a smile. "We love you. It's all going to be ok."

"I'm praying, Mom. I'm praying." *Too bad I already prayed for something else…*

Chapter 20

There were sleeping bags and suitcases all over the church parking lot. Excited youth were darting from one car to the other as seating arrangements were being made. She was still waiting on Jacob Grayson and his group. Once they arrived, she'd gather everyone into a circle to pray before heading off.

"Rachel!" Violet walked up and held out a paper. "This parental permission slip still needs to be signed."

"You've got to be kidding me!" Rachel took the paper and looked at the blank spot where the signature was supposed to be. "Great, I'm going to have to go to my office and see if I have another one on file from last year. I know the mom and she specifically asked me for this form on Sunday. She must have gotten distracted and forgot to sign this." Rachel started walking toward the church. She stopped mid-step and turned back to look at Violet.

"Thanks, Vi! Glad you caught this. And thanks for watching the kids out here until I get back."

"No problem, that's what I'm here for. I just wish I could go with you this year!"

"I know! But you've already been a huge help and I appreciate it!"

Rachel turned back toward the church and started walking again. She was almost to her office when she heard a familiar noise. Frank's truck was speeding by the church, windows rolled down and stereo blasting. When he neared the stop sign at the corner, he slammed on the brakes causing his tires to squeal. He'd made so much noise, the youth who were standing in the parking lot all stopped talking and looked to see what was going on.

Even though there was no oncoming traffic, he sat at the intersection for a long time and Rachel wondered if he knew she was watching him. She was uncertain of what she should do. While she didn't want to give him the satisfaction of knowing he held her attention, she didn't want to go into her office for fear he would start harassing her students while she was gone.

When he finally decided to drive away, he took off so fast his tires spun on the pavement, leaving a thick layer of rubber on the road. Rachel shook her head when she heard various comments from the youth. As she unlocked the church building and walked inside, her own thoughts couldn't help but echo the question the students had been asking.

What was that all about?

• ◦ ● ◉ ● ◦ •

The first few days of camp passed in a whirlwind of activity. The camp always had great things planned for the students who came, and they even offered times during the week when the counselors and youth directors could take some time off.

Thankful for the break, Rachel hiked the trail into the woods and found a beautiful spot near the lake. She was sitting with her back against the trunk of a tree, thinking and praying when the snap of a twig startled her.

"I'm sorry! I didn't mean to scare you!" Jacob Grayson laughed.

"Shame on you! I must have jumped a foot off the ground!" Rachel looked into Jacob's green eyes and pretended to scold him.

Jacob asked as he sat down. "May I join you?"

"It looks like I don't really have a choice," Rachel joked.

"You're right." Jacob smiled at her before he continued talking and she noticed how white and even his teeth were. "I've been meaning to tell you, I find it amazing how large your youth group is. How do you do it?"

"It's taken a while, but I think it has really just been God's blessing," Rachel said with genuine humility.

"Well, it's obvious that God is blessing your ministry. But I know that you've worked hard, harder than most youth directors do."

"I don't know about that," Rachel shrugged her shoulders. "I have a passion for youth. And when you have a passion, well, things work."

"How did you know youth ministry was something you wanted to be involved in?" Jacob reached out his right hand and picked a little wildflower. After a moment's inspection, he started spinning the stem between his fingers.

"I guess it had a lot to do with my own teen years. I grew up feeling pretty lonely. I was homeschooled and a pastor's kid. It doesn't get much worse than that, if you're looking to be popular." Rachel closed her eyes and shook her head; a small smile touched her lips. "I knew what God wanted me to do, but I also had a hard time with feeling so different. So now that I've seen how blessed I am to have followed God's plan for my life, I would like to help teens know that being different can be good. It's hard, but so rewarding."

Rachel looked over at Jacob and watched as he twirled the daisy in his fingers. His hands were big and calloused.

"What about you? What made you want to be a youth director?"

Jacob turned and looked at her with his piercing green eyes. "My reason is much the same as yours. I grew up in a Christian home as well, but I went to public school. I can't tell you how many times I was made fun of for having higher standards than everyone else."

"Tell me about it! When I decided not to casually date, everything got so difficult. People just didn't understand what it was all about. I simply want to save my heart, and body, for the man God has for me."

"I'm sure there were a lot of people who were upset by that decision," Jacob mumbled.

Rachel was surprised by his comment. "I'm sorry, but why did you say that?"

Jacob threw the flower down on the ground and shifted his weight. Awkwardness settled over him and Rachel wondered what had caused the change. There was a long stretch of silence while he seemed to be lost in thought. Finally he turned back to her and she noticed he was blushing.

"Because you're beautiful," Jacob said simply.

Rachel was just about to respond when they heard the dinner bell ringing. *It's probably for the best. I can't be in a relationship right now anyway. I have to get Frank to leave me alone first.*

* ∘ ●◉● ∘ ∘

Frank hated it when Rachel traveled. Even though they hadn't talked much lately, just knowing she was across the street made him feel closer to her. If things turned out okay in court, maybe he could start spending time with her again. He was certain that once she saw her parents' true colors, she would come running to him.

In the meantime, he needed to learn more about her. With paper and a pencil, he got in his truck and drove to Rachel's favorite place—the beach. Sitting in his truck and looking out at the waves crashing on the sand, Frank began to plan.

"She loves the ocean. I should ask her to walk on the beach with me," Frank said to himself as he started to write.

"Friends, who are her friends... " Frank realized he didn't know as much about her as he thought he did. He could only think of two people who were her friends: Violet and that Jacob guy. He knew for sure that Violet didn't like him. And Jacob was probably Rachel's friend for the same reasons he was, and that made him competition. Frank closed his eyes and sighed. *There has to be a way to get her away from her friends and family. She's too loyal to them.*

Frank spent hours at the beach that day and by the time he was ready to go home, he had pages and pages of notes. He had thought about everything possible. Now all he had to do was use all that information to form a plan.

 ⋅ ◦ ◉ ◦ ⋅

"I'd like to thank everyone for giving me the chance to speak this morning," Rachel said as she looked at the camp director. "I know we're all packed and ready to go home, but let's try to make the most of this time together. I want to share a bit of my story with you. I was just sharing with someone yesterday how I grew up being a pastor's kid. That was hard sometimes, but as I've gotten older, I see how blessed I am to have had such a unique childhood. I'm not going to take a lot of time to talk about my difficulties, but I want to share with you about the choice I made when I was your age." Rachel had shared this testimony with countless groups, and each time she shared it, she got the same reaction. After her next sentence, there would be a couple of kids who would snicker, a few who would gasp, and many who would look at her as if she were crazy.

"I chose not to date." Rachel paused, letting the crowd settle down before she continued. "I know for many of you, that choice is weird and extreme. And to be honest, it felt that way to me too, but that's what God asked me to do."

As Rachel was scanning the crowd, her eyes met Jacob's. For the briefest moment, she forgot what she was going to say next. There was something about him that was special, but now wasn't the time to think about it. Forcing her mind to focus, she started the next portion of her devotional.

"I don't know what God is asking of you today. But what I do know... is that unless you follow God's plan for your life, you won't find true happiness. When I stepped out in faith and told God I would follow His plan, I wasn't sure I would be happy." Rachel laughed a little. "But I realized real quick that the plan I wanted, my selfish plan, wasn't going to make me happy in the long run. Listen, if you don't remember anything else that I say to you this morning, please remember this: you will never be truly happy when you are outside of God's plan for your life. You may feel happy for a while, but it won't last. Lasting happiness is a gift from God, and you receive that gift by following His direction in your life."

Rachel motioned to the people who had volunteered to hand out the Bibles. "When you get a Bible, I want you to turn with me to Psalm thirty-four, verses one through five."

To the sound of pages turning, Rachel said, "While I wait for you all to find that passage, I'm going to tell you something about following God's plan for your life. It's something that I've learned and recently have been reminded of. Are you listening? Here we go: following God's plan is not easy. Let me say it again; following God's plan is not easy! It's going to be hard. There will be people who don't understand. There will be people who act as if you have a big sign on your back that reads "I'm different, make fun of me." And there will also be times when following where God leads will be dangerous. But the passage of scripture that has helped me a lot is the one you have looked up. Let me read it for you, while you follow along in your Bibles:

> 'I will extol the LORD at all times;
> his praise will always be on my lips.
> I will glory in the LORD;
> let the afflicted hear and rejoice.
> Glorify the LORD with me;
> let us exalt his name together.
> I sought the LORD, and he answered me;
> he delivered me from all my fears.
> Those who look to him are radiant;
> their faces are never covered with shame.'

"The first few passages say exactly what I am saying to you this morning; I'm asking you to praise God with me. It doesn't matter what we left at home when we came here. It doesn't matter what we are going to face later today when we get home. The praise of the Lord should be on our lips.

"But the second part of this passage is really what I want to talk about. When I stepped out and told God I would follow Him even though His plan sounded crazy, I was afraid. I was afraid of being so different than others. I was scared that I would be lonely, that people wouldn't want to be my friend. But when I talked to Him about it, He helped me to look past those fears. He showed me that His plan was best. Now, I'm confident that this passage of scripture is true; whatever God calls you to do, it will leave you radiant and shameless. You can always hold your head high when you are in God's will."

When Rachel closed her Bible, she saw many teens close theirs as well. Grateful that they had been so attentive, she took a moment to look around the room. *Lord, please help them to grasp this message. Help it to change their lives!*

"I'm going to do something a little different than I normally do. I'm going to ask our awesome band to come up on the stage and play softly for us. And while they play, I want each of you to ask God to show you where He wants to lead you today."

With the first strum of a guitar, Rachel closed her eyes. She was deep in prayer when she felt a touch on her hand. Looking up, she saw a young girl with tears in her eyes.

"Pray with me," the teen whispered.

As Rachel reached out and grasped the girl's hand, she saw a youth leader coming down the aisle with another girl.

By the time Rachel finished her prayer, there were students kneeling all around the room. *Thank you Lord, thank you.*

* ◦ ◦ ● ◦ ◦ ·

Each mile Rachel drove towards Casper filled her with sadness. Leaving the beautiful campground was always hard for her, but this time, leaving the peace and serenity was almost torturous. Frank was waiting for her and so was the arraignment. She had no idea what to expect, but she knew that attending the arraignment would cause her to be in the same room with Frank. And the thought of being so close to him made her ill. The only consolation was that she would be leaving for Portland, Oregon in just a few days and while she would only be gone two nights, at least the conference would provide yet another respite from the drama Frank was causing.

Just when Rachel was starting to get angry about the circumstances waiting for her at home, God reminded her of the message she had just shared. Feeling almost embarrassed, she chided herself for allowing her fear to speak louder than God's promises.

As Rachel drove, she tried to tune out the laughter and noise of the girls in the back seat of her car. She was deep in thought about the topic she would be teaching on in Portland when her ears honed in on a name.

"Isn't that Jacob guy cute?" one of the girls giggled.

"Shhhh, Rachel will hear you," another whispered.

"But he is cute. The girls at his church are so lucky! I'd be at church every Sunday if he was my teacher!"

Rachel couldn't stop the smile that spread across her face. *I wonder what they would say if they knew he called me beautiful...*

* · * * ● * * ·

Rachel was shaking. It didn't matter how many times she told herself she was a strong person and could handle anything that came her way, she was still shaking. Walking into the courthouse, Rachel had been overwhelmed with fear. But the emotion that bothered her most was the feeling of guilt. *Why do I feel like I did something to make this happen?*

Rachel quickly found a seat and waited with all the other people gathered in the room. She watched as one by one people would walk up to the window where a judge was seated. The judge would then inform the person of the charges against them and when they would appear in court. While Rachel was taking in her surroundings, Frank walked through the door and took a seat across the aisle from her. Seeing him almost made her panic, but there were police all around and she knew she was safe.

It felt like she had been there for hours when Frank's name was called. As he walked up to the window, she thought her heart would beat out of her chest. When the judge told Frank he was being charged with five counts of criminal stalking, Rachel felt a rush of emotions. At first she felt a sense of validation; if he was being charged with criminal stalking, that meant she wasn't overreacting. But just as quickly as the pleasant feeling of being right flooded over her, it left. In its wake was the stark reality that she truly was being stalked, and when she left the courtroom today, he would, too. There was nothing to keep her safe.

The court date was set for the second week of December which meant she had close to four more months of waiting. Thankfully, Frank was issued with a temporary stalking order; while that should have given her peace of mind, she knew Frank would be angry and there was no telling what he would do in his anger. *Anything can happen in four months! Lord, please protect me!*

Chapter 21

"Thank you so much for driving me to the airport!" Rachel said as she relaxed in the passenger seat of Violet's car.

"You're welcome. I still can't believe Frank is being charged with criminal stalking! That's crazy, Rach."

"It is. I feel like I'm stuck in a bad dream. I just hope these next four months go fast."

"Well, it's almost September already. And you'll be gone a few days for this conference, so that will help."

"Yeah, it will probably go faster than I think it will."

Violet turned and looked at her friend for a brief moment and smiled. "You know... that Officer Sinclair is really cute!" Violet giggled and Rachel's jaw dropped.

"Are you serious? I hadn't even noticed. Besides, I thought you wanted me to get to know Jacob."

"No, Silly! I meant for me! He's handsome and nice and he's a hero for goodness sakes. What girl wouldn't want that?" Violet's grin was huge and Rachel's heart warmed at the sight. Violet hadn't smiled like that since before she went to Mexico.

"Oh, I see. Well, he has committed to helping out with youth group, so there will definitely be more chances to get to know him."

"Speaking of Jacob, have you decided I'm right?"

"Right about what?" Rachel laughed.

"That he's perfect for you!"

"Oh my, here you go again. I suppose you're going to tell me again how our names matching the Bible story mean it's meant to be." Rachel rolled her eyes. "But he did call me beautiful… "

"He what? Why didn't you tell me sooner?" In her excitement, Violet almost swerved into the other lane. "Give me the details!"

· ◦ ◉◉ ◦ ·

The words the judge had said repeated over and over in Frank's mind. For days he'd been shocked and angry that he'd actually been charged of doing something wrong.

"I'm not a criminal stalker!" He yelled at Phil. It was Monday morning and Phil would soon leave for work. Frank, on the other hand, had nothing to do today except stew over his circumstances.

"You've been saying that for days now," Phil said as he finished his bowl of cereal. "Why don't you get a job and quick mooching off of me? If you worked, you wouldn't have so much time to be stalking that girl."

"I'm not stalking her! She's my future, can't you understand that? If it wasn't for her parents trying to control her, we'd be together." Frank was pacing now. His large bowl of cereal sat forgotten on the table.

Phil didn't say a word. He simply stood up, walked out the door and drove away.

He just doesn't understand. I'm not sure he even has a heart. Probably doesn't know what it feels like to love someone.

Frank wandered around the house looking for something to do. Maybe Phil was right, maybe he should get a job. Some days he was so bored he actually wouldn't mind working again.

With a sigh, Frank walked to the front window and looked out at Rachel's house. Everything was quiet. Dew was sparkling on Rachel's car, the drops of water added to the depth of the paint, making the red stand out even more against the black. He was amused by the changing color of the car and stood at the window for a long time, moving his head back and forth ever so slightly. The car turned from black to red and then back to black, depending on the angle he looked at it.

I wish I could ride in that car again! I wish she would ask me out on another date.

Feeling depressed, Frank walked into the kitchen and opened the refrigerator. Moving aside a gallon of milk, he grasped a bottle of beer. He normally preferred his beer in a can, but the bottled had been on sale and with his lack of employment, money was getting harder to find. He rummaged in a kitchen drawer to find an opener. He smiled in amusement as he ripped the cap off the bottle and watched the bent cap bounce off his bare foot before hitting the floor. *There's nothing like a cold beer in the morning.*

One beer turned into two and two turned into more. Before he knew it, he was drunk. For the hundredth time that day, he walked to the window and looked out. He was hoping he'd see Rachel, but she still hadn't come out of her house.

With nothing else to do, Frank decided to stay at the window and wait for her. While he waited, he remembered all the reasons why he loved her. Then, as if his memory had brought her to life, she walked out her front door. Frank's heart started pounding as he watched her walk across the street to stand in his yard.

"Frank! Frank! I want to talk to you." Rachel was waving at him. "I can see you. Just come on out and we can talk. You don't have to worry about the stalking order; my parents probably won't see us talking."

Frank opened the window so he could talk to her. "Rachel, I don't want to chance it. Can we just talk from the window?"

"No, Frank, we can't. You have to come out here. How else could I trap you into getting arrested?" Rachel was looking at him as if he was an idiot.

"What happened to you? You've never had such an attitude with me?"

"What happened to me? I'll tell you if you come out," Rachel laughed. "I'm sure the police would like to arrest you for bothering me."

On and on Rachel harassed him. He tried closing the window and walking away, but she just stood there laughing and when he didn't come back, she started throwing rocks and sticks at the house, trying to get his attention. It was enough to drive him crazy!

I've got to get another beer; that will help.

With legs that weaved with too much alcohol, he stumbled his way to the kitchen. Upon discovering he'd run out of beer, he cursed and punched the refrigerator. Crying out in pain as he shook his hand, he cursed again, picked up an empty bottle and chucked it to the floor. Glass scattered across the room as the bottle shattered. He could still hear Rachel taunting him and was filled with a fresh wave of anger. His anger propelled him into action—he was going to go outside and confront her!

He was almost through the kitchen door when he stepped on a large piece of the broken bottle. Screaming in pain, Frank looked down to see a large cut. He picked up the glass and saw blood smeared on one of the jagged edges.

With the bloody glass in one hand and his injured foot in the other, he hopped back into the kitchen to find a bandage. When he was just one or two more hops away, the room started to spin. He felt himself start to tip forward and put his hand up to break the fall. With the bloody broken beer bottle still clutched tight, he placed his hand on the edge of the kitchen table, but his body weight was too much for his drunken arms to support. He lurched forward, hit his head on the table and then crumpled to the floor. Blood streamed down his face and dripped into his mouth. He wiped at his mouth and looked up. Sure enough, he could see red glistening on the edge of the table.

The combination of seeing his own blood and being drunk joined together and caused him to lose consciousness. As the darkness closed in on him, he could still hear Rachel yelling accusations at him.

When Frank woke up an hour later, he couldn't remember how he got on the floor. Sitting up, he saw the blood on the broken bottle and table. When he tried to stand, searing pain told him there was something wrong with his foot. He walked to the table on his tip toes and pulled out a chair. With the clumsiness that always told him he'd consumed too much alcohol, he sat down and rested his hurt foot on the table. While the cut looked like it needed stitches, it had already scabbed over enough to stop the bleeding.

"What happened?" he said out loud. And as the words came out of his mouth, he felt a scab tear open on his cheek. Reaching up with shaking fingers, he touched his face. *More blood. Why can't I remember what happened?*

Knowing he needed to have the cuts looked at, Frank started to make his way to his truck. When he opened the door and stepped out of the house, he stopped and stared at Rachel's car parked in the driveway across the street. Memories of Rachel standing in his yard flooded his mind and anger filled him.

Moving as fast as his inebriated, wounded legs would let him he went into the house and picked up the phone. After dialing 911, he waited impatiently as the phone rang. By the time the operator answered the call, Frank was livid.

"What took so long for you to answer? This is an emergency! I need the police to come out right away."

"I'm sorry sir. What is your address?" yhe operator responded in a professional tone.

"7092 Ocean Heights Drive."

"And what is your emergency?"

"I'm being threatened and harassed by my neighbor!" Frank yelled. "I was knocked unconscious and when I woke up, I saw blood. She hurt me!"

"All right, sir, try to calm down and I'll send an officer right out."

* ◦ ● ◦ •

When Frank saw the police car park in front of his house, he limped outside and stood on the front porch, being careful not to put too much weight on his injured foot. Frank watched as Officer Shawn Sinclair opened the car door and stepped out. Frank cursed. *Just my luck, they send out the guy who has the hots for Rachel.*

"What seems to be the problem?" Shawn asked as he drew close to Frank.

"Rachel was standing in my yard, yelling at me. When I opened the door to ask her to leave, she came running at me. All I can remember is her forcing the door open and it hitting me in the face." Frank pointed to the gash in his cheek. "I guess I was knocked unconscious, because I woke up lying on the kitchen floor. Next to me was a piece of a bloody beer bottle and my foot's all cut open."

Shawn was looking at Frank as if he didn't believe a word he said. He carefully looked at the cut on Frank's face and then asked to see his foot.

"Mind if I take a look inside?" Shawn said after he examined Frank's foot.

Frank didn't answer, but simply stepped aside so Shawn could enter. After seeing the bloody beer bottle and table, he came back out and looked around the yard.

"All right, I'm going to have you fill out some paperwork." Shawn handed Frank the forms and a pen. "I'm going to go talk to Miss Riley. Have those ready for me when I come back."

· ⦾ ⦿ ◉ ⦿ ⦾ ·

Shawn knocked on the door and waited. There were a million thoughts running through his head and most of them centered on how absurd Frank's story was.

"Officer Sinclair! Is something wrong?" Mary gasped when she opened the door.

"Mrs. Riley, can I talk to Rachel?"

"I'm sorry, she's not home. She flew to Portland a few days ago to speak at a conference. She won't be home until tomorrow. Is there something I can help you with?"

Shawn vacillated between relief that Rachel was out of state and anger that Frank would come up with such a bold-faced lie.

"No, Ma'am. It's just that Frank Smith called and said there was a disturbance. He claims Miss Riley came into his yard and was harassing him. He's sustained some injuries and was trying to blame her."

Mary's eyebrows shot up and she turned pale. "No one will believe him will they?"

"I hardly think so. Rachel is small and no match for a man his size. He's drunk, it's obvious that he was hallucinating and I'm going to put that into the report. His story doesn't add up, and there's no proof to back up what he's claiming. No need to worry."

"Thank you, I'm glad we have someone to count on through all of this!" Mary sagged in relief. "Let me know if you need any more information."

"I will. Have a good day!"

Shawn walked back across the street to collect the papers from Frank.

"What did she have to say for herself?" Frank asked with a triumphant look.

"I wasn't able to speak with Miss Riley as she is out of state right now," Shawn told him. "Are you sure you want to press charges? The way I see it, you have no grounds. There's no proof whatsoever that Miss Riley was here today. Are you absolutely certain that she was here? There's no blood on the door. You are obviously drunk. I believe it's in your best interest to drop this. In fact, you should just drop the whole thing, I'm getting pretty tired of this and I'm just about to show you what it feels like to have someone harassing you! You better stay away from her and if I ever catch you on her property or at her church, you'll wish you had never started this."

"Are you threatening me? Of course I'm pressing charges! She's accused me of stalking and then she comes over here harassing me and hurting me!" Frank shook his fist at Shawn. "You just want me to drop this because you don't want any more trouble for Rachel. You may be in love with her, but she was mine, first!" Frank threw the papers at Shawn, walked into his house and slammed the door.

Chapter 22

The months until the court date loomed before Rachel with uncertainty. If Frank was desperate enough to call the police and make up a story about her, what else might he do?

Rachel had only been home from Portland for a week, but if felt more like a month. Since she had returned, Frank seemed more determined than ever to annoy her with his presence. He would drive around the block several times every day with windows down and music blaring. It didn't matter if it was raining, cold or foggy; at 7:00 every morning, Rachel would wake to the sound of his truck. It was a horrible way to start each day and Rachel longed for an escape.

Just when Rachel was wondering if life would ever return to normal, Frank seemed to disappear. Although she had no idea why he stopped making his presence known, Rachel was grateful for the change.

It was now the end of September and Rachel longed to go to the park and enjoy the fall weather while she studied. But even though Frank had been absent from her life recently, she had no idea where he was or what he was thinking. Knowing the only place she was truly safe was either at home or in the presence of others, Rachel settled for sitting by her bedroom window to admire the colors of fall. She held in her hands her old beat up dictionary and her worn leather Bible. She also had a list of topics she wanted to teach the youth about. Glancing at the list, she tried to decide what she was going to study and got distracted by a misspelled word. *What is wrong with me? I can't even remember how it's supposed to be spelled! I've got to be less focused on Frank. I'm too distracted these days.*

Just as Rachel was opening the dictionary to look up the correct spelling, the phone rang. Thankful she had thought ahead to bring the cordless phone upstairs with her, she picked it up and looked to see who was calling. After the last phone call from Frank, the Rileys made sure they had caller I.D. added to their phone. And she was glad, the last thing she needed was a disturbing call while her parents weren't home. Rachel didn't recognize the number, but since it was a Fort Bragg area code, she decided to go ahead and answer.

"Good morning! Riley residence, this is Rachel." Years ago, her parents had taught her to answer the phone this way. And now that she was grown, it came in handy since her voice sounded a lot like her mother's.

"Good morning to you, Rachel! It's Jacob Grayson from Fort Bragg Baptist."

"Hi Jacob, how are you doing?" The quiver of excitement that his voice gave her left her surprised.

"I'm doing well. Say, I was wondering... I know it's really last minute, but would you be interested in going out to dinner tonight? I was hoping we could talk about some of the special youth events coming up."

Go out for dinner? Is he asking me on a date or is this strictly ministry related?

Rachel hesitated for just a moment before throwing caution to the wind. "Sure, I'm available. Just tell me when and where."

* ⸱ ● ● ⸱ *

Frank couldn't believe what he was seeing. When he followed Rachel and Dan to Fort Bragg, he had no idea she was going on a date. Dan had driven Rachel to a local eatery and then drove off. Watching her walk into the restaurant and greet that Jacob guy was almost more than he could take. He was instantly filled with jealousy and anger. *And she told me she doesn't date! She's a little liar.*

Frank watched Jacob and Rachel the whole time they ate dinner. It was painful to see Rachel enjoy spending time with another man. She had never looked that happy when she was with him, and the thought almost drove him crazy.

When they were finally finished with dinner, Jacob walked Rachel to his car and gave her an awkward hug before they got in. Just seeing her in Jacob's arms set his heart racing and he clenched his jaw to keep from yelling. He'd deal with Jacob later; for now he needed to remain unseen. If anything else was going to happen between them, Frank wanted to know about it.

Much to Frank's relief, they pulled out of the lot soon and it looked like a clumsy embrace was all that Jacob was going to get from her. Frank debated for a moment whether he should follow them or not. Figuring Jacob was probably just going to take her home, Frank decided to take a detour and stop by the store to replenish his beer supply instead of tailing them.

• ◦ ●◉● ◦ •

Rachel had been home for about a half hour when she realized she hadn't fed Shadow. The poor dog had gone all day without any food! The night air was cold and Rachel didn't feel like going out again, so she just opened the front door and called for him through the screen door. Shadow was nowhere to be seen and Rachel wondered where he was.

"If you escaped again, I'm not going out there to find you. You've got one more chance and you'll just have to wait until morning to eat." She yelled even though she knew he wouldn't understand her.

The sound of her voice must have gotten his attention, because she suddenly could hear the bell on his collar jingling. He had been over at the neighbor's house and as

Shadow began to cross the street, a car was heard speeding down the road. In mere seconds, the headlights glared on the pavement and Shadow appeared to be in a spotlight.

"Go, Shadow! Go!" Rachel held her breath as she feared her dog would be run over.

Just before the car would have hit him, Shadow darted to safety in Rachel's front yard. The driver of the car slammed on the breaks; and then, with a jerk on the steering wheel, pulled the car up to the front of Rachel's house and parked. She gasped when she saw the driver. Frank was driving a different car! The weight of what this meant settled on her shoulders and she suddenly turned cold. Frank hadn't stopped following her, he'd simply out-smarted her. Somehow, whether he had purchased, borrowed, or stolen it, he'd gotten another vehicle!

Furious, Rachel watched Frank step out of the car and walk to the trunk. Shadow ran up to him and started rubbing and jumping at Frank's legs.

"You're a stupid dog!" Rachel muttered. "You're such a traitor..."

Wanting to stay unnoticed, Rachel tried to see what Frank was getting out of his trunk. The screen door was in her way and she was just about ready to move to a window when Frank stepped away from the old, beat up car.

Rachel felt a hot wave of panic wash over her and dizziness made the room spin. *Don't pass out, don't pass out!* What happened next only took a few seconds, but Rachel felt as if everything was in slow motion.

As she watched in horror, Frank pulled a gun out of the trunk and took a few steps away from the car. Then, with a look that was filled with hate, he pointed the gun at Shadow and pulled the trigger. Shadow fell to the ground before the sound of the shots stopped ricocheting against the houses.

Frank quickly threw the gun into a garbage bag. He picked up the limp dog and tossed him in, too. Tying off the bag, he placed it in the trunk. After slamming the trunk shut, he peeled off the gloves he was wearing.

Rachel was frozen in place. She watched in silence as Frank drove away. Information was swirling in her head. Frank had a car. He had probably been watching her all these weeks. Frank owned a gun. Shadow was dead.

Chapter 23

Rachel was numb. The police were in her house and she was being questioned, but she couldn't think straight. All she could say was, "He killed my dog. I saw him, he killed my dog!"

Mary had wrapped Rachel in a quilt and was trying to calm her down while Dan took the police outside to talk. Since Frank had taken the body, there was no evidence to prove that Rachel was telling the truth. And until the body showed up or they found a way to prove Frank was guilty, there was nothing they could do about it. The police officer had also said that Frank wasn't in violation of the temporary stalking order because he hadn't harmed Rachel.

Rachel wished it was Officer Sinclair who had come in response to the call for help. The man who came out didn't seem to care. He acted as if Rachel was being silly. But she knew this was more than just the death of a dog. This was a warning—a sign.

Mary convinced Rachel to sit down on the couch and rest. As the warm quilt chased away the cold, the numbness wore off. Fear and grief tore at her heart and Rachel rocked back and forth as she sobbed. For the first time in her life, she felt small and helpless. No longer was she the strong woman she prided herself in. Instead, she was a terrified little girl.

When Dan came back inside after the police drove away, the sight of his sobbing daughter caused his face to crumple in pain. With quick steps, he walked to her and wrapped her tight in his arms.

"Oh, Daddy. I'm scared. I'm so scared!"

"I know, sweetheart. I know. I'm going to call my sister and see if you can go stay with them until the trial. Everything will be fine. Don't you worry."

* * ● * *

The days spent in Texas with her aunt's family were enjoyable and Rachel tried to make the best of the situation, but the fact that she had fled her hometown bothered her. She wasn't worried about the youth group; Violet would do a fine job of filling in for her. In fact, it might even be a good thing for Violet since Shawn had committed to help out, too. Everything had been taken care of and for that, Rachel was grateful. But she chafed at the idea that Frank had won. He had caused her to back down and she wasn't acting like the strong woman she wanted to be; she was acting like the scared woman she was.

With many phone calls to her parents and to Violet, Rachel stayed connected to her loved ones while she was away and the time passed quicker than she had anticipated. With a knot in her stomach, she boarded the plane that would take her back home.

◦ ◦ ●◉● ◦ ◦

Dan pulled the car into the driveway that rainy December afternoon and Rachel was surprised to see Violet's car parked in front of the house. When she walked into the house, Rachel was thrilled to find Violet and her mom standing next to Mary and Grandma Ruth. They had made a hand painted "Welcome Home" sign and her favorite cake was sitting on the table. Rachel couldn't stop the tears from flowing down her face. It was so good to be home!

After long, teary hugs from everyone, Rachel sat next to her grandma at the table and smiled while Mary began to cut the cake.

"Well, the trial is just one week from today. Praise the Lord it will be over soon!" Dan said as he sat down at the table. "Come on, join us and make yourselves comfortable." Dan waved at Violet and Cora.

As the women took a seat, Mary passed out large slices of gooey fudge cake.

"I still can't shake the feeling that all this started with something I did. I mean, why choose me, why not go after someone that actually likes him?" Rachel shook her head.

"I think you may be right. I think it is something that you did." Violet surprised everyone with her comment. "Let me finish. I think it's because Rachel has chosen to be different than most people her age. And the things he's said to her tells me that it's her uniqueness that makes him want her."

"That's true, I can't tell you how many times he's told me that I'm different and he likes that."

"Wait a minute," Mary held up her hand to interrupt. "I see what you are saying, Violet, but I'm learning that violence is never the victim's fault. It's normal to feel we've done something to deserve it or make it happen, but there's no reason whatsoever for violence, threats, or anything like that. He could admire you and respect your wishes at the same time."

"Thanks for sharing that, Mary. I guess it just goes to show that standing out from the crowd can be more difficult than we thought, and for many different reasons," Cora said as she reached out and placed a hand on Violet's arm. "I know that both these fine girls suffered through gossip and disapproval from their peers while they were in school, and now all this!"

"I have to say, I don't miss my high school days at all!" Violet laughed.

"It was hard. Everyone seemed to be going down the same road and when we stood up and said we wanted to travel down a different one, it was like we had committed a crime." Rachel looked at Violet and remembered the difficulties of answering God's call to be set apart. "Oh, but I'm glad I had you to support me, Violet!"

Violet smiled and noticed the tears that threatened to spill from Dan and Mary's eyes. "What does all this stalking stuff mean? And what do we do now?" Violet asked with sadness.

There was a long period of silence as each person pondered the question. Rachel knew the answer; she just didn't want to share it with everyone. *It means God heard my prayer and I have to face what I asked for...*

"It means we press on," Dan spoke into the silence. "What Frank intends for evil, God can use for good. The way I see it, Rachel will have a great opportunity to witness."

Mary looked at her husband with love, and then she turned to Rachel and gave her a loving look as well. "And just like when your peers tried to bring you down, you need to hold your head high and stay focused on God. You'll make us proud. I know you will. And Rachel, remember what we learned at that meeting? You're not alone; women are harassed and abused all the time. And they've all had the same feelings of shame and guilt you've struggled with. But you know the truth, sweetheart. You can teach others how secrecy and self-blame fuel this kind of stuff."

"You're right, Mom. It may be part of our society to look the other way when women are suffering, but maybe I can use my situation to change that."

"But first," Violet said with tears in her eyes, "you need to think about your own safety. Then you can go save the world."

Chapter 24

Frank was once again enjoying some beverages at his favorite bar. But this time, he had more on his mind than using alcohol to wash away his troubles. Tonight, he was looking for help. With the trial just one week away, it was time to get things in order.

Sitting at a table with a beer in one hand, Frank looked around for an easy target. After assessing the character of the women present, he decided to hone in on the blonde two tables over. She wasn't exactly pretty, and the way she was throwing herself at the men who were near her told him she would be easily flattered. And manipulated.

Taking one last swig of beer, he stood up and walked over to her table.

"I couldn't help but notice you from across the room." Frank poured on the charm.

The blonde giggled and patted the seat next to her. Frank sat down and when she put her hand in his lap, he was taken off guard for a moment, but he quickly recovered and began flirting with her. Frank was confident he'd made the right choice; her boldness could work in his favor. With a smile, Frank set his plan in motion. *This is going to be easier than I thought.*

· ◦ ● ◉ ● ◦ ·

Shawn had been on his rounds for several hours and was ready to head back to the station when he saw something strange. Instinctively, he slowed the car down and looked all around to see if there was any danger. Nothing looked out of place.

Why is that woman just lying in the road?

With caution, he pulled his car to the curb and stepped out. He had one hand on his gun, ready to shoot if the need arose. As he drew closer to the woman, he recognized her. She'd been taken in many times for soliciting. And while he detested the thought of what she did, his heart couldn't help but feel compassion for her. There were many reasons a woman ended up in her situation, and most of the time it wasn't her fault.

The woman appeared to be unconscious, so Shawn reached down and checked for a pulse. Thankful that she was alive, he gently shook her to see if she would wake up. With really poor acting, she pretended to regain consciousness. *What is she up to? I can tell she's faking.*

"Oh! Officer! I'm so glad you rescued me! She's after me. She tried to kill me. And all because she's jealous of me." The woman rambled on and on.

"Ma'am, I don't know who you're talking about," Shawn said patiently.

"That Rachel woman. I think her last name is Riley."

"Why don't you sit up and you can tell me all about it." Shawn held out his hand and the woman took it. He pulled her up into a sitting position, but quickly moved away from her as she tried to throw herself into his arms.

"She crashed in on me and my boyfriend. She was all crazy and wild. She was yelling at me that he was hers and I better stay away." The woman turned her big blue eyes towards Shawn and batted her eyelashes. "I can't help it if all the men want me."

Shaking his head in disgust, Shawn stood up and started to walk away. But after a few steps he stopped. He knew the woman was lying, but he also knew he couldn't just drop this. He either had to make this woman admit she was lying, or he would have to report this. Failure to handle this properly could result in losing his job.

"Look Ma'am," Shawn said as he turned back towards her. "I think that both you and I know you're lying. Now I don't want to have any trouble and neither do you. Are you sure you want to start talking to the law? I imagine there are a lot of things you'd like to keep secret from the law right now."

The woman looked at Shawn defiantly, and then without warning, she crumpled to the ground and started crying.

"I didn't want to do it. But he said he'd hurt me if I didn't help him." She was sobbing now and Shawn had to strain to understand what she was saying. "I don't know Rachel Riley, never seen her."

"Who said they would hurt you?"

"A guy I met at the bar."

"If I showed you a picture, do you think you could identify him?"

With a single tear running down her face, the blonde shook her head. "Yes, I can."

＊ ◦ ◉ ◦ ＊

Frank was standing in the shadows, watching the whole scene play out. How many times had he warned her not to talk to Officer Sinclair? That woman wasn't worth his time! And now, it looked like she had just made things worse for him.

Frank kicked a rock, and then cursed as it made noise. Reminding himself to be quiet, Frank slowly turned and walked away. Things weren't going well for him. With Rachel's reputation being so solid, he was bound to lose the trial. If he lost, then all his dreams would be lost, too. Phil had told him to just give up, that even if he won the case Rachel would never be his. But Frank wasn't ready to give up. There had to be a way to make her love him. Rachel was not the type of person you met every day. She was different. She was his destiny and he wasn't going to give up on her.

＊ ◦ ◉ ◦ ＊

"Grandma, would you like some more tea?" Rachel asked, holding the tea pot near her cup.

"Yes, please, that would be wonderful. I'll take one of those cookies, too."

Rachel was reaching for the plate of cookies and jumped when the phone rang. *Goodness! I'm so flighty. This trial has me on pins and needles...*

Rachel glanced at her grandmother as if apologizing, then walked away to answer the phone. After a quick glance at the caller I.D., she picked up the phone and greeted the caller a good afternoon.

"Rachel! It's Jacob. I just talked to your dad and he said you were back in town. Did you have a nice visit with your family?" Jacob was cheerful like always.

"I did, thanks for asking." Rachel wondered how much her father had told him. "How have you been?"

"I've been just fine. But I have been tired of waiting on something."

"Oh, and what's that?"

Jacob laughed. "On you! I've been waiting to take you to the botanical garden. I hear they decorate it with Christmas lights this time of year and I would love to see it."

Rachel wasn't sure if she should be happy that he was asking her to go with him. Wasn't her life complicated enough already?

"So what do you say? Do you want to go?"

Unable to resist the handsome pastor, she smiled, "What about tomorrow night? Will that work for you?"

Chapter 25

"Of course it had to rain tonight!" Rachel said as she stepped into Jacob's car.

"Oh, it's not that bad. And besides, a little rain never hurt anyone," Jacob smiled and winked at Rachel, causing her to blush.

"I don't know. I might melt. I'm made out of sugar, didn't you know?"

Jacob laughed and started the car. "You are sweet, but I still think you can handle a little rain. Besides, didn't you grow up on the coast?"

"I did. And seriously, rain never bothers me."

The two rode in companionable silence, each content to just be in good company. And when they arrived at the botanical gardens, they were pleased to see the rain had dwindled down to a light mist.

They paid the entrance fee and entered the park, noticing how few people had braved the rain to come look at the lights. After just two steps into the large garden, Jacob stopped and stared. Thousands of lights were wrapped around trees and shrubs. A rainbow of colors beckoned people to explore each trail that led into the heart of the vast garden. Rachel watched with enjoyment as he took in the lights. Seeing his look of wonder caused her to realize how much she had taken this beautiful place for granted. *When you come every year I guess it's easy to forget just how special it is.*

"This place is huge!"

"Yeah, I think it's around three acres. The first time I came at night I thought I might get lost," Rachel laughed.

"Let's go find a place to sit and take it all in." Jacob grabbed her hand and tugged her down a path. The feel of his fingers wrapping around hers made Rachel's breath catch. Jacob led her through the park, commenting on a light display here and there. Finally they came to a secluded place with a bench.

Jacob grinned in delight and pulled her to the bench. "This is perfect!"

She was acutely aware of his closeness when they sat down and in spite of the cold breeze, Rachel felt overly warm. Not knowing what to do or say, she forced herself to look at the scenery.

"There's something I want to talk to you about," Jacob said softly.

Rachel turned her head and looked at the man beside her. The soft light danced around them and covered them with a feeling of intimacy. When their eyes met, she knew. She had tried to avoid what was happening, but it was no use. Whether it was the right time in her life or not, she knew she was falling in love with him. Violet was right. Jacob matched every requirement on her list of what she was looking for. From his love of ministry to his captivating green eyes, Jacob Grayson appeared to be the man she'd been waiting for all these years.

"What... " Rachel tried to still the tremble in her voice. "What did you want to talk about?"

Jacob smiled and leaned toward her. The added closeness allowed Rachel to smell the spicy scent of his cologne and it was almost intoxicating.

"I've been praying a lot since I met you and I feel... "

Whatever Jacob was going to say was completely lost on Rachel. Someone walking by had caught her attention, causing all other thoughts to flee. The little hairs on the back of her neck stood on end and panic set in. Before Rachel knew what she was doing, she stood up.

"I can't stay here! You have to take me some place else," she whispered frantically.

"Rachel, what's the matter?" Jacob looked at her with concern.

Without any explanation, Rachel grasped his hand and pulled. Jacob got to his feet and allowed her to drag him towards the exit.

"Rachel, I'm sorry... maybe I was out of line... " Jacob was confused.

"It's not you!" she hissed. Rachel was running now. She had a death grip on Jacob's hand and forced him to keep up with her. "I'm not safe here! Get me out of here!"

As soon as she said she wasn't safe, Jacob started sprinting. Rachel was relieved that he seemed to understand and ran as fast as she could alongside him. With the cheerful Christmas lights marking their path, it was easy to see where they needed to go. The problem was, the rain had left patches of slippery mud and both Rachel and Jacob had to slow down for fear of falling. Every now and then, Rachel would hear a twig snap and wonder if it was their feet that broke the twig, or Frank's.

They rounded a corner and were about to reach the main path when all of a sudden Jacob went down. Unable to let go of Rachel's hand fast enough, he pulled her down with him. Rachel screamed as she fell on top of Jacob and then rolled off into the mud.

"Are you okay?"

"Just help me up!" Rachel said in a hushed voice, struggling to her feet. "Get me out of here!"

Jacob reached out took her hand again and helped her stand. When she tried to take a step, she cried out in pain.

"Darn it! I was afraid of that." Rachel looked at Jacob with fear in her eyes. "I hurt my ankle. I can't run."

Jacob didn't give her a chance to say anything else. He simply grabbed her by the waist and threw her over his shoulder. Had Rachel not been so scared, she would have been embarrassed. But right now, the only emotion she had was relief that Jacob was taking care of the problem.

Rachel closed her eyes for a brief moment and prayed for their safety. After she finished her prayer, she opened her eyes and saw a glimpse of him. Frank was following them!

The sight of her stalker caused Rachel to scream and Jacob, not knowing what was going on, stopped running.

"Go! He's following us! Go!" she urged quietly.

Jacob started running again, this time at a frantic pace. Minutes later, they arrived at the car.

As soon as they neared the car, Rachel said, "I'm fine. Just put me down and get in!"

Jacob looked at her as if questioning her plan, but when he saw her successfully hopping into the car, he did as he was told. With a turn of his wrist, Jacob started the car. He released the parking brake and put the car into reverse all at the same time. With a look behind him, he quickly backed out of the parking space, and then stopped to shift into drive.

"There he is! Hurry!" Rachel screamed, locking her door.

Jacob finished shifting into drive and stomped on the gas pedal. The engine revved, but the vehicle didn't move.

"Great, we're stuck in the mud!"

"No! We can't be!" Rachel was crying.

"Get into the back seat, maybe the extra weight will be enough to make the tires catch."

Rachel quickly obeyed and climbed over the seat. As soon as she sat down, Jacob tried again and they both cheered as the car lurched forward. Rachel looked out the back window and watched as Frank ran behind their car for a while before giving up. When he stopped running, Rachel sagged against the seat.

"Please take me home," Rachel said in a weary voice. "Just take me home."

Jacob drove faster than he should have, but Rachel didn't care, she just wanted to get away from Frank. With each mile they drove, Rachel grew calmer.

"I'm sorry I freaked out on you," Rachel said after she climbed back into the front seat.

"Would you care to tell me what that was all about?" Jacob looked at her and she noticed he had mud caked on his chin.

"I think that's only fair." Rachel was glad he was driving. Maybe she wouldn't have to make eye contact. "I wish I didn't have to say this, but I do."

Jacob's silence caused her to look at him. Seeing that his eyes were on the road and not her, she turned and gazed out the window.

"I'm afraid of what you might think," she said softly.

"Come on, Rachel, don't you know you can trust me?" Jacob's expression told her he was hurt. But he quickly masked it with a smile, and then a joke. "It's not every day that I carry a muddy woman over my shoulder. I think I proved that I'm a hero. And heroes are definitely trustworthy."

Rachel couldn't resist laughing. This man was good for her. He had the ability to take a terrible moment and turn it around.

"All right then, I'll just get right to the point." Rachel closed her eyes and sighed. "I have a stalker. And I'm going to court next week."

Jacob's face told her he wasn't expecting the news she had just told him and before she lost her nerve, she kept going.

"I feel guilty, like I did something to cause it. I'm ashamed Jacob, even though I know it's not my fault."

"Do you know who he is?" Jacob asked through clenched teeth.

"Yes. He's my neighbor. In fact, you met him. At the time, he was claiming to be related to me."

"I remember being annoyed at the way he looked at you." Jacob lifted a hand and ran it through his hair. Cussing, he slammed his hand back down on the steering wheel.

"Okay..." Rachel laughed. "That's not the response I was expecting."

"Sorry." Jacob looked embarrassed. "It just makes me so angry that this guy is doing this to you. I'd like to teach him a thing or two."

"Jacob, I didn't tell you this to make you angry... " Rachel hesitated, not certain what to say. "I just, I just don't want you to think I'm some weirdo."

"I would hardly think that. I may not know you as well as I would like to, but the Rachel I know is very level headed. She's also strong and confident. And that's what makes me so angry. There was panic in your eyes back there and it broke my heart to see it."

"So you're not ashamed of me? You don't think I did something to make all this happen?" Rachel could barely get the words out.

Jacob looked at her tenderly and said, "I know beyond a shadow of doubt that you didn't make this happen." Then he reached out, took her hand and drew it up to his lips. The kiss thrilled her, but the guilt inside her stole away her joy.

If he knew the whole story, he wouldn't be saying that. If I wasn't so afraid of his rejection, I'd just go ahead and tell him.

Rachel moved her fingers ever so slightly and Jacob tightened his grip as he brought them away from his mouth. *But for now, the prayer stays a secret.*

Chapter 26

Frank watched as person after person walked into the courtroom. Knowing the growing group contained the six people who would make up the jury was unsettling. He watched them intently, hoping these people wouldn't be biased towards Rachel.

The arrival of Rachel and her parents caused the crowd to hush for just a moment. Looking at her, she appeared to be calm and collected. But Frank had watched her enough to know when she was upset. And today, she was definitely upset. *Good. Maybe she'll regret calling the police and making all this happen.*

Once the bailiff ushered the judge into the room, the long process of selecting the jury began. When the judge asked if anyone knew either Frank or Rachel, several people said they knew the Rileys and respected them. So they were dismissed. The second question, concerning personal experience with stalking, resulted in several more people being dismissed. When all the requirements had been met, there were still a dozen people to choose from.

Frank missed how the selection was made; he was distracted by Rachel. Seeing her sitting across the room messed with his mind. While he stared at her, he told himself to get it together. If he was going to make it through this trial without being convicted of a felony, he needed to be focused.

The sound of the judge dismissing everyone brought Frank's attention back to the jury. It would appear that the job was finished. The five men and one woman standing before him would hold his fate in their hands.

⁕ ⁕ ◉ ⬤ ◉ ⁕ ⁕

"I just don't see how a jury of five men is fair!" Rachel raged as they drove home.

"It's in the Lord's hands, Sweetie, you've got to trust that this will all turn out ok."

"Mom, I know what you are saying. But I'm sorry. That just doesn't help right now."

"It's okay to feel angry and upset," Dan said. "But ultimately, you've got to be still and know that God is in control."

The drive home seemed long and exhausting. Even the beautiful scenery couldn't soothe Rachel's frayed nerves.

"It's ridiculous that we have to drive to Fort Bragg every day. I didn't ask for this trial! Why do I have to do this? Why can't Frank just leave me alone?" Rachel picked up her purse and threw it across the car. "I hate the way he looks at me! I don't think I can stand to be in the same room with him. He's such a jerk. I've never met anyone that was a bigger jerk!"

Rachel's tantrum went on and on. At one point, Mary started to say something, but Dan reached out and touched her arm to stop her. "Just let her get it out," he whispered.

By the time they reached home, Rachel was quiet. She'd said everything there was to say about the situation. With resignation weighing her down, she stepped out of the car and started to go in the house.

"Rachel! Wait," Mary said, running up to her daughter. "Look over there."

Rachel was done feeling ornery, and now she was just tired. With a sigh, she looked to where Mary was pointing. It was then that she finally saw him. Jacob was sitting in his car with the windows rolled down and he was looking at her with a smile. When their eyes met, he waved. Then he quickly got out and stepped to the rear passenger door of his car. Rachel watched with curiosity, wondering what he was doing. For a long time, he stood there with his back to her. Then, with the largest grin she'd seen on his face, he turned around. In his hands was a giant bouquet of red roses.

Enjoying the moment, Jacob walked slowly to where she stood. When he was near enough, he reached out his arm and offered the flowers to her.

"I thought your day might need something beautiful in it."

"It was, ah... " Rachel had to swallow to stop the tears that threatened to fall. "It was a horrible day." She took the roses and buried her face in them. The heavy, sweet fragrance seemed to wash away the stress. "Thank you. These are wonderful."

Jacob looked at her with serious eyes. "Would you like to talk about it? Or would you rather we just sit out here on the porch and discuss the weather?"

"The weather?" Rachel laughed. "Can't you think of something less boring?"

"I don't know; I bet I could come up with something worse... " Jacob started to laugh, but quickly got himself under control. With a serious face, he turned to her and said, "In fact, I was just reading this book on youth ministry... "

"You're awful! My book is not boring!" Rachel punched him in the arm. As she quickly walked up the steps she said, "If you'd like to wait while I put these roses in water, I could give you a lesson on manners when I come back."

"I'll be right here," Jacob smiled and took a seat.

Rachel hurried to find a vase, filled it with water and went back outside. She found Jacob sitting on the top step of the porch. His long legs were stretched out and he looked relaxed.

"Feeling right at home, I see." Rachel said as she sat next to him.

Jacob was serious, all the playfulness from before had vanished and Rachel wondered what had happened.

"I got a subpoena," he sighed.

"Jacob, I'm sorry." Rachel shook her head. "If I had known you would get all mixed up in this, I would never have gone to the garden with you."

"I'm not sorry. I was just wondering how you felt about me being there. I know neither of us have a say in whether I go or not, but I still want to know how you feel about it."

Rachel looked into his eyes and uncertainty filled her heart. "I... I don't know what Frank is going to say about me. For that reason, I'm not sure I want you there." Feeling too vulnerable, Rachel broke eye contact and looked at the ground.

"Rachel. Look at me." Jacob waited for her to do as he asked, but she didn't. Taking her chin gently in his hand, he tipped her face up until their eyes met. "I don't care what Frank says about you. I know the truth. Do you understand that?"

With tears filling her eyes, Rachel nodded her head *yes*.

"Good. I'm glad that's settled." Jacob took his hand from her face. "You know, if we left now, we could probably catch a beautiful sunset at the ocean. A little more beauty in your day couldn't hurt could it?"

Chapter 27

The trial had begun. As the jury was gathered and the witnesses prepared to go before the judge, a fierce wind blew outside. Every now and then lightning would light up the sky, followed by booming thunder. Rachel thought the storm mirrored the raging emotions inside her. Fear of Frank clashed with her faith in God, resulting in a restlessness that shook her from her head down to her toes. She wanted to run. She wanted to stand up and scream at Frank. She wanted all this to be over.

With pain twisting in her stomach, she watched as first her mother and then her father were questioned by Frank's lawyer. Chris Silverstone was arrogant and condescending, but good at his job. It didn't matter what either of her parents said, he always found a way to turn it around for Frank's benefit.

The District Attorney, Paul Grant, was acting as Rachel's lawyer and had already questioned Dan and Mary. And with growing discomfort, Rachel realized he wasn't as well prepared as Mr. Silverstone. As Frank's lawyer tore apart her parents' testimony, he quickly disputed any points Mr. Grant had previously made. Rachel turned and looked to where Violet and her mother were sitting. With a pale face, Violet smiled and nodded to her, trying to encourage Rachel. But she knew that Violet was just as concerned as she was.

When Shawn took the stand, Rachel held her breath. Surely this would change the way things were going.

After he was sworn in, Mr. Grant asked Shawn a series of questions and when he felt confident that he'd made his case, Mr. Grant turned Shawn over to the defense.

And just like with her parents, Mr. Silverstone wasted no time. He dug into Shawn like a starving wolf ripping into its prey.

"Officer Sinclair, when did you first meet Miss Riley?" he asked.

"I first met her when her father called the police in July."

"And did you know her before then?"

Shawn looked annoyed. "Like I said, I met her for the first time in July."

Mr. Silverstone raised his eyebrows as if questioning the truth of the statement. "And did you find Miss Riley to be attractive?"

"Objection, Your Honor that is not relevant to the case!" Mr. Grant yelled.

"Objection overruled," said Judge Gainsley.

Mr. Silverstone nodded to the judge, and then turned back to Shawn. "So did you find her attractive?"

"I was more focused on my job than I was on the appearance of Miss Riley." Shawn answered with a nervous look.

"Is it true that you put in your report that Miss Riley fits the stereotype of someone likely to be stalked?"

"Yes, I did."

"And just what exactly does that mean?"

"Well, from my experience, the victims are normally well-known. And they are often small or petite."

"But not attractive?" the lawyer smirked.

Shawn hesitated. "Uh, yes, I suppose that could be seen as an element."

Mr. Silverstone turned and looked at the jury as if he had made a point. With a glance in Rachel's direction, he said, "I think we could all agree that Miss Riley is indeed beautiful."

Shoving his hands into the pockets of his slacks, Mr. Silverstone took a few steps toward the stand. "Mr. Sinclair. Is it true that you have been attending Miss Riley's church every Wednesday?"

"No, sir. Sometimes I work on Wednesday nights."

"But when you are not working, would you be found there?"

"Yes, I would."

"Is it not true then, that you have developed a relationship of sorts with Miss Riley?"

Shawn looked from Mr. Silverstone to Rachel, and then back to the lawyer. "I'm not sure what you are asking?"

"You're not?" Mr. Silverstone asked condescendingly. "It's pretty simple. Do you or do you not have a relationship with Miss Riley?"

Paul Grant was on his feet the moment the words came out of Mr. Silverstone's mouth. "Objection!"

"Objection overruled!" the judge said.

Shawn looked at the judge as if hoping he'd change his mind. But when the Judge told him to answer the question, he knew he had no choice. "Yes, you could say we've become friends."

"Just friends?" Mr. Silverstone looked bored. "Are you sure there is nothing more to your desire to be around Miss Riley? Are you sure you have not been given sexual favors in return for your taking Miss Riley's side in this case?"

"Absolutely not!" Shawn slammed his fists on the wood railing of the witness stand. His anger was apparent.

"Objection Your Honor!" Mr. Grant was just as angry as Shawn was.

"Objection sustained." With a look of annoyance, the Judge said, "Mr. Silverstone, watch yourself!"

Mr. Silverstone looked up at the judge with faked humility. "I'm sorry." When he saw the District Attorney smile in victory, he said, "If you were merely just friends, then why would this situation with Miss Riley cause you to go outside your bounds as an officer? Didn't you threaten to personally harm Frank if he were to set foot on church property?"

Shock rolled through Shawn as he remembered that moment of anger, the need for justice to be meted out. With a look of embarrassment, Shawn cleared his throat and said "I simply pointed out that harming Rachel, or any of her students, would be a major indiscretion."

"Your Honor, I request that Officer Sinclair's testimony be disregarded. Due to the relationship he admitted to and to his trying to take the law into his own hands, I believe he has a conflict of interest, and therefore his police reports may be biased."

The judge looked as if he were having a hard time deciphering the accuracy of the conflict of interest. But with a sigh, he said, "Request granted. Let the jury strike the testimony of Officer Sinclair."

With a look of gloating, Mr. Silverstone turned to Shawn and said, "Officer Sinclair, you are dismissed."

. ◦ ◦ ● ◦ ◦ .

When the trial was dismissed for the day, Shawn flagged Violet and Rachel down as they walked to their cars.

"Violet, Rachel, wait!" he yelled across the parking lot.

Upon seeing Shawn, they stopped walking and waited for him to catch up. Rachel glanced over at her car and saw her parents patiently waiting. When she caught their eye, they nodded their heads and mouthed the words, "Take your time." In return, she smiled at them and turned to greet Shawn as he approached.

"Rachel, I'm sorry."

"Shawn, it's not your fault." Rachel reached out and touched his arm. "That Silverstone guy is tough!"

When Rachel touched him, Shawn's eyes went to her hand and she could see his discomfort. Feeling awkward, she pulled her hand back.

"So… uh… I feel like I need to clear something up now." Shawn was looking at the ground. But when he looked up, it was Violet's face he turned to, not Rachel's. "Violet, I have been going to the church for more than the teens. I've been going because of a beautiful woman whose heart I'm hoping to win."

Violet stood silent and completely still, but her eyes were begging him to continue.

"Violet, it's you. You're the reason I'm at the church. Please don't let this botched testimony make you think my heart is elsewhere."

"Thank you for clearing that up," Violet whispered, her eyes brimming with tears. "Rachel is beautiful…and I… well… "

Shawn didn't give her a chance to finish her statement; he took a step closer to her, wrapped his arms around her waist and pulled her into a kiss.

Chapter 28

"Hey, I'm sorry I had to leave so soon after we were dismissed yesterday," Jacob said as he walked Rachel into the courtroom the next day. "I had wanted to tell you not to worry. That was just the first day, and just because things didn't go so well, it doesn't mean that today will be the same."

Rachel had to quicken her steps to keep up with his long strides. "I certainly hope you're right."

When Jacob opened the large wooden door into the courtroom, he placed his hand on the small of her back and guided her inside.

"Where are your parents?"

"Oh, they were running late, so I had to leave without them." After they found a seat, Rachel looked at her watch. They still had a few minutes before court was in session again. Not knowing what the day held made her nervous. She would have preferred being able to know when she was to testify. But for some reason, no one could tell her when that would happen.

"Jacob, can you pray for me?"

Without a word, Jacob reached out and took both her cold, trembling hands into his large, steady, warm ones and started praying.

* ∘ ● ∘ *

"Miss Thompson, would you please tell me what happened the day you and Rachel were driving to the beach?" Mr. Grant asked.

Violet was the first to take the stand that morning, and she was doing a fantastic job. She was clear and precise, and the jury seemed to be hanging off her every word.

"Yes sir;" Violet said, "we were driving to the beach when Rachel started to panic. Rachel, who is normally very level headed and calm, was very agitated and upset. She said that we were being followed."

"I see," said the District Attorney. "And were you, in fact, being followed?"

"Yes, I looked back and when I did, I could see we were being followed."

"And do you know who was following you?"

"Yes, it was Frank Smith. He followed us until we decided to turn around and go home." Violet closed her eyes for a brief moment as if trying to recall the events of that day. "We pulled off Highway 1 and turned around at Garden View Road. While we were waiting for traffic to clear so we could get back onto Hwy 1, he pulled up next to Rachel's car. He got out of his truck and started yelling at us."

"Do you remember what he was yelling?"

"No sir, I don't really remember. I was really scared and so was Rachel. All I remember was helping Rachel stay focused on driving."

"And why did Rachel need help driving?"

Violet's eyes filled with tears as she looked at Rachel. "Because she was terrified."

◆ ◦ ◉ ● ◉ ◦ ◆

When Mr. Silverstone walked up to cross examine Violet, Rachel looked at Jacob with fear in her eyes. Every time this man talked to a witness, things looked better for Frank.

"Miss Thompson, did you say Mr. Smith frightened you?"

"Yes." Violet's voice was loud and clear.

"And why would you feel that way about a man you don't really know?"

"I may not know him very well, but I've seen enough of him to know that he isn't nice."

"Again, what makes you feel that way?"

"Rachel told me she saw him beat up his brother." Violet looked at Mr. Silverstone with defiance. "And he shot her dog."

"That's hearsay, Miss Thompson. Do you have any first-hand knowledge of Frank being mean?"

"I saw the way he acted when he followed us. Anyone would have been able to see how agitated we were, but he didn't care. In fact, he appeared to enjoy our fear."

"Miss Thompson, it hasn't been proven that Frank's intentions were ill. Are you sure there isn't some reason you may be paranoid of men?"

Surprise and confusion were evident on Violet's face. Rachel glanced from Violet to Mr. Silverstone, trying to figure out where he was going with his questioning.

"Is it true Miss Thompson, that you were kidnapped recently?" he pushed, trying to get an answer from her.

Paul Grant was yelling out his objection, but Rachel didn't notice. All she noticed was the pain that flashed across her friend's face. *How does he know about that?*

"Objection sustained." The judge said. "Miss Thompson's personal life is not relevant to this case."

"With all due respect Your Honor, I feel that it is. Her experience may have changed the way she sees men, therefore changing the way she would interpret Frank's intentions."

"Mr. Silverstone, Objection sustained!"

With a smirk, Frank's lawyer dismissed Violet. It was apparent that he didn't really care that Judge Gainsley didn't agree with him, he was satisfied with simply having placed doubt in the jury's mind concerning Violet's testimony.

◆ ◦ ◉◉◦ ◦ ◆

It had been a difficult day for Rachel. After watching Jacob testify about the incident at the botanical garden, she had to sit there and watch as he too was ripped apart by Mr. Silverstone. Once again, the lawyer had found a reason why the testimony wasn't enough proof--Jacob had never seen their follower that night. He had simply reacted to Rachel's fear.

When Jacob walked down from the stand, he came and sat down next to Rachel. It was almost as if he knew who was to testify next and wanted to offer his support. When Frank Smith was called to witness, Rachel reached out and held Jacob's hand. With each step Frank took toward the stand, Rachel's grasp grew tighter.

The District Attorney, Paul Grant, asked Frank a series of questions, each one building on the next. And when he felt the jury was ready, he brought the letters out. With a flourish, he waved them in front of Frank.

"Do you recognize these?"

"Yes, sir, I do. I wrote them to Rachel," Frank said.

"And why is it that you wrote to her and said that you loved her?"

"Because she was pursuing me strongly and I thought she wanted a relationship." Frank paused and then looked at Rachel. "She did ask me to go on a date. And when we were on that date, she was throwing herself at me. I actually had to tell her to stop because we were in public and I was getting embarrassed."

The words made Rachel's stomach churn as anger and disgust washed over her and she thought she was going to be sick. A wave of heat spread through her body, and she broke out in a cold sweat. Looking around, she made an exit plan just in case she couldn't calm the churning of her stomach. She was embarrassed enough by what Frank had just said; she didn't need the added humiliation of vomiting in public.

"That's interesting, because all the witnesses before you have claimed that it's you who has been doing the pursuing. Who's telling the truth?"

"Are you calling me a liar?" Frank challenged.

Mr. Grant took a step closer to the stand. "I'm simply observing the fact that the information doesn't add up. But since you brought it up, did you tell Miss Riley and her family that you are related?"

Rachel watched with satisfaction as Frank paled. Apparently he was hoping this wouldn't get brought up.

"I did."

"And why would you do such a thing?"

"Rachel's Grandma told me about her niece who was given up for adoption; I thought I would look into it because Ruth's niece had the same name as my stepmom. For a while there, I had gotten some information which confirmed my thoughts that I was related, but later on I was told by the adoption agency that it was a mistake."

"I guess we'll have to trust you on that one." Mr. Grant looked at the jury and Rachel wondered if he too was hoping they could see that Frank was lying.

Lie after lie was told and by the time Frank left the stand, Rachel couldn't hold her head up. She could only look at the floor. She was so embarrassed by the things Frank had said about her. As everyone left the courtroom for the lunch break, Rachel wished she could hide instead of sit there and watch them pass by. But for some reason, she couldn't make herself move. Her arms and legs felt heavy, as if all the shame she felt was weighing her down.

Violet placed a hand on Rachel's shoulder. "Come on Rachel, let's go get some lunch." Violet, along with her mother, had walked over to where Rachel was sitting with Jacob and her parents. "Some food will make you feel better."

"I don't think I can eat," Rachel whispered. "I'm ruined. My reputation is ruined."

The little crowd that was gathered around her looked at each other, each hoping the other had some words of encouragement that would break through her grief. But when no one spoke, it was apparent they were all at a loss for words. Dan cleared his throat and made an effort to remove the tears welling in his eyes. Then, with a voice that cracked from emotion, he led the group in prayer.

As Rachel listened to her dad pray, she started to feel strengthened. And when he quoted her favorite verse, she felt her shame lift away. *Okay, God, I'm looking to you just like the Psalmist said in Psalm 34. Make me radiant instead of ashamed.*

* • ◉ ● ◉ • *

The moment she'd been dreading had finally arrived. As she made her way to the witness stand, it was as if time stood still. In the minute it took her to walk the short distance, she noticed how the hardwood floor creaked with each step. She saw a layer of dust on the heavy drapes and wondered why no one had taken the time to clean them. Her nose registered the smell of furniture polish. And as she sat down in the hard chair, she realized the courthouse was really old. *I wonder how many victims have sat in this chair. Where they all just as scared as I am?*

When Mr. Grant started questioning her, Rachel was grateful that she could trust him. There were no trick questions; no need to worry about what he was going to ask next. He was simply helping her unfold her story in a way that was easy to understand.

But when Mr. Silverstone began his cross examination of her, the stress was almost more than she could bear. She was close to tears when he asked his first question.

"Miss Rachel, have you dated very many people?"

"I've never actually dated anyone." Rachel wished she could sound more self-confident.

"And why is that?"

"Because I believe God has someone special for me and I want to keep my heart for only him."

"Or is it because your parents don't want you to date?" Frank's lawyer challenged.

"Like I said, I've chosen not to date because of my personal convictions. While my parents support my choice, they are not the ones who caused me to make that choice. I'm simply following God's plan for my life."

"Could you tell us how old you are?"

"I'm twenty-two."

Mr. Silverstone smirked. "And you want us to believe that you have never dated or been in a relationship."

"I'm simply stating the truth, sir. I would hope our society hasn't gone downhill so much that finding someone my age who is taking a stand for purity seems unbelievable."

Rachel watched in victory as Mr. Silverstone appeared to be taken off guard by her statement.

"Miss Riley... uh... you have testified that you are afraid of Frank. But I feel like there is more to the story. Why are you afraid of him?"

"Because he won't leave me alone, the more I ask him to stop pursuing me, the worse it gets."

"And your lack of experience with relationships has not caused you to misinterpret his intentions?"

"This has nothing to do with my choices concerning dating." Rachel had to restrain herself to keep from yelling. "It has everything to do with Frank and his choices."

"Miss Riley, has Frank ever threatened you?"

"He has repeatedly asked to get me alone."

"But has he specifically said he wants to harm you?"

Knowing that he was making a very good point, Rachel simply shook her head no.

Mr. Silverstone paced between the jury and the witness stand. "Miss Riley, did Violet's kidnapping have an effect on you?"

Rachel closed her eyes for just a moment. *I knew this was going to happen!*

"Miss Riley? Did you hear the question?"

"Yes. It scared me. I would hope that most people would feel just as much concern upon hearing of a kidnapping."

"Would you say that the experience has caused you to see Frank in a different light than you might have otherwise?"

"No!" Rachel blurted out. But knowing it wasn't the complete truth she said, "Maybe."

"Would you care to clarify?"

"I was concerned about Frank before Violet was kidnapped and I think I would have felt the same concerning his actions regardless, but I... I... " Rachel started to cry.

Looking first at the jury, then back at Rachel, Mr. Silverstone said, "Please continue."

With a ragged breath, Rachel whispered the words, "I said a prayer."

"I'm sorry, I'm not sure we all heard you," he said condescendingly. "What did you say?"

"I prayed! All right? I prayed for all this to happen. That's why I'm so frightened by him."

Chapter 29

The moment the words were out, Rachel regretted them. She looked out at the crowd and saw her parents wipe tears from their faces. Violet's eyes were filled with tears, too, and Jacob's jaw was set in an effort to hide his emotion.

But the person who seemed the most affected by her words was Frank.

"That's not relevant! Who cares about a prayer?" Frank yelled as he came running toward the witness stand. "That means nothing! I object! Make her shut up!"

Rachel gripped the seat of her chair and braced herself, not knowing what Frank was going to do. The bailiff ran toward Frank, but Jacob got there first. With anger flashing in his eyes, he grabbed Frank by the shoulders and slammed him to the ground.

"Get off of me! I wasn't going to do anything!" Frank yelled.

Placing a knee in his stomach, Jacob lowered his face until it was inches from Frank's ear. Rachel watched with a pounding heart as Jacob whispered something before the bailiff took over. Jacob stood, looked at Rachel for a moment and returned to his chair.

Once Frank was ushered back to his seat, Judge Gainsley said, "Mr. Smith, must I remind you that you are on trial here? And Mr. Grayson, if you are to remain in my courtroom, you will stay seated. If either of you get out of your seat or say another word, you will be charged with contempt of court." After seeing both men nod their heads in understanding, he turned and looked at Rachel. "Miss Riley, please continue your testimony."

A lengthy amount of silence stretched out before Rachel's unsteady voice said, "Your Honor, when I heard that Violet had been kidnapped... I... I instantly thought she might be... " Rachel looked at the floor, not certain she was able to share such a personal thing with so many people. *I can do all things through Christ who gives me strength.* The words flitted through her mind, leaving her with a boldness she didn't have before. "I thought she was going to be raped. That's what normally happens in kidnappings. I love Violet and I would never want such a terrible thing to happen to her. So I... I asked God to make it happen to me instead."

Mr. Silverstone actually had a look of compassion as he asked, "And what would cause you to believe that this prayer was being answered?"

"Because soon after I prayed, Violet was found. And she was safe and unharmed."

"But how does that imply Frank's intentions are for harm?"

"Well, I had actually forgotten about the prayer until I realized that Frank kept saying he wanted to get me alone. Then I noticed that he was always watching me. It seemed like every time I went outside he was there, staring at me." With a look that begged for understanding, she made eye contact with Frank's lawyer. "Sir, maybe you don't understand what it feels like to be small. But I'm just a little over five feet tall. Frank, on the other hand, is over six feet and anyone can see that he's very muscular. I would be lying if I tried to deny the fact that if Frank wanted to, he could easily overpower me. If he decided that he wanted to rape me, I would be defenseless against his strength. Tell me, would that not place fear in your heart?"

"I... uh... I suppose it would," Mr. Silverstone cleared his throat.

Rachel looked at the jury and said, "I just want him to leave me alone. Is that too much to ask?"

After glancing at the judge, Mr. Silverstone looked at his feet for just a moment before he said, "Miss Riley, you may be excused."

• ◦ ● ◉ ● ◦ •

Feeling confident in Rachel's testimony, Paul Grant rested his case. It was now time for Chris Silverstone to bring out Frank's witnesses.

Rachel watched in amazement as Mr. Silverstone produced several people who claimed to be friends with both Rachel and Frank. These witnesses, all of whom Rachel had never seen before, told the court how Frank was a gentleman and Rachel was nothing more than a love-struck girl who wanted him. Rachel lost count of how many times Mr. Grant objected to their testimony. And with a sinking heart, she knew it didn't really matter anymore. It was simply Frank's word against hers. The outcome rested on whether the jury believed the truth or the lies that were being told.

When both the District Attorney and Frank's lawyer finished their closing arguments, the jury left to deliberate and everyone was asked to stay close by in hopes that a verdict would be decided upon soon.

During the wait, Rachel found herself sitting on a hard bench in the hallway by the courtroom. She was surrounded by her parents, Violet and her mom, and Jacob. They were all quiet, each lost in their own thoughts. Some attempts were made at small talk, but no one felt like talking and soon silence reigned among the group.

After what seemed like hours, they were informed that the jury was ready to announce their verdict. Rachel walked on shaky legs into the courtroom. She was flanked by Violet and Mary, followed by Cora, Dan, and Jacob. She held her head high, and praised the Lord that this long, tortuous trial was almost over.

Once everyone was seated, the jury walked single file into the courtroom. One by one, they stood in front of their chairs. When the last person arrived at his chair, he looked at the others and they all nodded at him. With a grim face, he opened the envelope he held in his hand. Withdrawing a small piece of paper, he held it up and read the verdict out loud.

"We, the jury, find Mr. Frank Smith not guilty of all counts of criminal stalking."

Chapter 30

The disappointment of losing the trial was hard to take; it settled over Rachel like a dark cloud, leaving her unable to think clearly. And while it was obvious that Frank was excited about the verdict, he remained silent. He simply looked at her and smiled before he walked out the door.

After hugging Violet and Cora and watching them walk away, Rachel turned to Jacob and shrugged her shoulders. There wasn't much to say other than goodbye.

"I guess I'll see you later." She said as she turned to walk away.

Jacob reached out and caught her arm. "Wait a minute! If Violet gets a hug, I should get one, too," he said with a mischievous smile.

Rachel looked at him for a long time. *Where does he fit into all this? Even though I could easily fall in love with him, can I trust him?*

Despising the fact that she felt so confused, Rachel walked into Jacob's arms. She was expecting just a friendly hug, but it turned into something more when Jacob tightened his arms around her while brushing his lips against her cheek.

"I know you're disappointed, I'm sorry. But I'm here for you, you can trust me," he whispered.

Rachel pulled back from his embrace just enough to look into his eyes. Feeling vulnerable, she looked away.

"I just need to go home and sleep," Rachel sighed. "Maybe things will feel different tomorrow."

"Okay, I'll talk to you later."

When she stepped out of his arms, she felt cold. Wondering why she felt such a sense of loss, she almost reached out to him. But she knew that her emotions were jumbled right now and it was best to wait until things calmed down before she made any decisions concerning Jacob. She'd guarded her heart for twenty-two years; a few more days wouldn't hurt anything.

After waving goodbye to Jacob, Rachel linked arms with her mom. With Dan following close behind, they walked out of the courtroom.

As they neared Rachel's car, they found Frank waiting for them. The shock of seeing him left Rachel breathless and trembling.

"What are you doing here?" Dan demanded.

"Oh, I'm just enjoying my freedom." Frank smiled at Dan and then turned and winked at Rachel. "I guess the jury didn't believe your story after all. Maybe you can quit acting and start telling your parents the truth now."

When Dan started toward Frank, Rachel reached out and grabbed his shirt sleeve. "Just ignore him. He's not worth our time."

Dan looked at Frank for a few minutes, and then said, "You're right. Let's go."

Laughing, Frank turned and walked away. "I'll see you at home!"

. . .

It had only been a few days since the trial, but Frank had already made it clear he wasn't going anywhere. Just like before, every time she went outside he was there.

With frustration, Rachel looked out the window. In her hands, she held her car keys and a shopping list. She had hoped she could leave without him noticing, but it appeared that he was watching for her. *Why doesn't he have a job or something?*

Her irritation grew, causing her to feel defiant and stubborn. "Who cares?" She yelled at him through the window. "I'm going to the store and I'm not going to let a jerk like you stop me."

With steps made confident by anger, she quickly walked out the door. As she was getting in the car, she heard Frank say her name. The sound of his voice grated on her nerves and she had to restrain herself from yelling at him to shut up.

The whole time she drove to the supermarket, she thought of all the names that fit a guy like Frank. As she parked, she rehearsed the different ways she wanted to use those names and in her mind's eye she could see his reaction. With an amused smile, she stepped out of the car and started walking toward the store.

"You're so beautiful when you smile."

Surprised, Rachel turned around and gasped. She had been so angry, she'd forgotten to look and see if he was following her. "Frank! Leave me alone!" Even though she had rehearsed, she still couldn't force the names past her lips. *I just can't lower myself to his level. I have to stay in control of myself. Be angry but do not sin.*

"I wish you wouldn't lie to me. I know you don't really want me to leave you alone. Let's stop pretending, okay?"

Without another word, Rachel ran into the store and started shopping. With a small grocery basket tucked into the crook of her arm, she stormed down the aisles. Every now and then she would look behind her, but he was nowhere to be seen. Feeling hopeful that he had gone away, she started to relax and by the time she was looking for the last item on her list, her heartbeat had returned to normal.

She was reaching out to grasp a jar of spaghetti sauce when someone tapped on her shoulder. With a startled scream, she turned around and swung the jar, hoping to protect herself.

"Wait! Rachel!" Violet said as she stepped back quickly. "Goodness sakes, you almost hit me!"

Sagging in relief, Rachel nearly sat on the floor. "Never do that again!"

"Hello, this is Officer Sinclair, how can I help you?"

"Hi, it's Rachel. Frank is following me everywhere." Rachel tried not to sound too panicked. "You've got to do something."

"Has he touched you or hurt you?"

"No, he never has. He's just always there. Every time I go out of my house, he's there."

"Rachel, I'm sorry. But there isn't anything the police can do. Since you lost the trial and you don't have a protective stalking order, we have no reason to stop him. Now if he hurts you, then that's a different story."

Rachel shook her head, not liking what he was telling her. "Well, how long do I have to wait until the paperwork goes through for the stalking order? It's been a long time already and the temporary one only lasted until the trial."

"Rachel... " Shawn let out a sigh. "I thought you understood. You haven't filed for a stalking order."

"What?" Rachel nearly shouted. "Then what did I sign that night when you came out to my house?"

"That was just the police reports. You've got to call the women's hotline and ask for someone to help you file for a stalking order. But, I'm really sorry to tell you that stalking orders are hard to get. And losing the case isn't going to help you any."

"Shawn, I have to do something! I can't just wait around for him to hurt me."

"I know. I understand, you definitely should file for the order, I just wanted you to know that it's hard to get one." Shawn paused. "There's something else you need to know. You can't rely on me as a police officer. You heard the judge; I supposedly have a conflict of interest. So if you need official help again, you've got to talk to someone else on the force."

"What? But I don't trust them like I trust you!"

"Rachel, I'm still here for you. I will come to your aid in the blink of an eye. But you need someone else to be filing the police reports. You need proof and it needs to be solid. Okay?"

Frustrated beyond words, Rachel agreed and said goodbye. What was she going to do? She was back to where she started. Only now, Frank was angry.

Chapter 31

It was a cold January day when Rachel walked into Jacob's office and sat down in the chair across from his desk. It seemed like it had been forever since she'd last seen Jacob, but in reality it had only been a few weeks. She looked around the room and tried not to eavesdrop as he ended a phone call. She laughed to herself as she realized that it didn't matter how many times she sat in his office, she was always amused by his expansive Spiderman collection. There were posters all over the walls, figurines on top of his bookcase, and he even had a life-size cardboard cutout in the corner of the room. With a sad sigh, she regretted not getting Jacob a Christmas gift. Picking one out for him would be easy; all she would have to do is find something to add to his Spiderman collection. But this year, Christmas hadn't felt the same. With Frank lurking around every corner, she had felt like a prisoner in her own home. And even though she knew she hadn't been rude, she was embarrassed that she hadn't thought to buy her friends gifts. Even Violet didn't receive a present from her this year.

"Sorry about that," Jacob said, bringing her back from her wandering thoughts. As he hung up the phone, he sighed, "Some parents are enough to make you regret being in youth ministry."

Rachel laughed, "I have to say I wholeheartedly agree. But if it weren't for those parents, there wouldn't be as big a need for people to minister to their kids. So I guess they are job security."

"You've got a point there," Jacob grinned.

"So where are you taking me to eat?"

"That sandwich shop downtown?" When Rachel nodded her head, Jacob stood up and said, "Okay. Let's go then."

After locking his office, Jacob walked with Rachel to his car.

"So how are things going with Frank?"

"Well, does the fact that my dad drove me here tell you anything?"

"I was wondering where your car was. It's that bad?"

Rachel stepped into the car while Jacob held the door for her. When she was settled, he carefully closed the door and walked to the driver's side and got in.

"It's been a long time since we've talked. A lot has happened." Rachel looked out the window to see if they were being followed; it was a habit that she had formed over the last year. She never knew when and where Frank would show up. "After the trial, Frank started following me everywhere I went. I called Shawn and asked him what they could do. But he said they can't do anything until Frank actually harms me. He also said that I should call someone else next time because of the whole conflict of interest thing."

"You've got to be kidding me! What about the stalking order?"

"It turns out that I never even filed for that. The papers I signed were simply police reports."

Jacob gripped the steering wheel and Rachel watched his knuckles turn white. A small shiver of pleasure coursed through her heart. *He's mad. He cares about me. But does he love me?*

"So I guess maybe that prayer… "

"Rachel! Stop." Jacob interrupted. "How can you possibly think God really works that way? It's as if He were some mystic genie and all you have to do is pray and you get what you ask for, even if it means harming yourself."

Rachel looked at Jacob for a while, and seeing how mad he was, she wondered if he was mad at her or Frank. "Look, I don't think God is a genie. If I did, I'd just ask Him to fix the whole world and get everyone freed from their problems. It was a simple intercessory prayer… and I think it was answered."

Jacob released his grip on the steering wheel and placed his hand on Rachel's knee. "I admire greatly that you would be willing to take on Violet's pain and suffering. But praying for someone's safety and believing you can take on a potential rape are two different things. I don't believe God works that way, and I don't think you understand what intercessory prayer is."

The words worked their way into Rachel's heart. Tears quickly formed in her eyes and unashamedly, she let them fall. With a radiant smile, she looked at Jacob. "You're right. Thanks."

When they pulled into the parking lot of the sandwich shop, Jacob parked and shut off the engine, but didn't move to get out. He turned in his seat, looked at Rachel and asked, "Is there really a conflict of interest? Is there something between you and Shawn?"

Surprised, Rachel raised an eyebrow and turned to look Jacob in the eye. Her forehead was crinkled in confusion as she said, "Do you really have to ask that?"

"I don't know, Rachel, we've never really talked about it."

Reaching out, Rachel took his fidgeting hands in hers. "I wouldn't be here with you today if there was something between Shawn and me." Rachel could feel him relax. "Besides, I talked to Violet yesterday. We've both been so busy we haven't connected in a long time," Rachel laughed. "But she told me why she's been so busy."

"And why is that?" Jacob asked.

"She's been spending all her time with Shawn! All she's been doing is dating him and working on her schooling. She hasn't even taken the time to answer my calls! I think she's pretty infatuated with him."

"Wow, she must be if she doesn't have time for you! I thought you two were inseparable." Jacob was grinning now. "But I guess that leaves you with more free time…"

Rachel knew where he was going to take the conversation, and while she was aware that she was falling in love with him, she wasn't ready, not yet. Frank was still in the way.

"So anyway," Rachel changed the subject, "I filed for the protective stalking order a few weeks ago and am now waiting to have a date set for that. It's not a trial or anything; it will be just Frank and me before a judge. No jury this time."

Jacob's smile vanished and he was once again serious. "What are you doing until then? You're not safe and that bothers me more than I can say."

"Well, I have made an effort to never be alone anymore. I only go to the church when my dad is there. If I need to go shopping, I take my mom. And if both my parents plan to be away from home at the same time, I go with them. It's a pain, but at least it keeps him away."

Jacob's expression was stern and Rachel could see the concern in his eyes. "If you need something, you'll call. Right?"

Rachel reached out her hand and touched Jacob's arm. "I promise. Thanks."

· · ●● ● ● · ·

Frank sat in his car outside the little sandwich shop where Jacob and Rachel were eating. They had chosen a table that wasn't next to a window, so he couldn't see them, but he knew they were in there. When they had walked through the door holding hands, jealousy boiled up inside, leaving him unable to think about anything other than getting Jacob out of the picture.

Knowing he had a long wait ahead of him, he pulled out the peanut butter and jelly sandwich he'd brought with him and took a big bite. After wiping some jelly off his face with the back of his hand, he reached for the can of beer he'd wrapped in a paper bag. In a few quick movements, he had the can open, and with a smile of satisfaction, he held the beverage to his lips. *There's nothing like a good beer with peanut butter and jelly.*

Once his sandwich was gone and his beer can was empty, Frank had reclined his car seat and put his feet up on the dash. Even though he was comfortable, he was growing impatient. How long did it take to have lunch anyway? He was contemplating whether he should stay and wait or just go on home. But then he saw Rachel and Jacob walk out of the restaurant.

The sight of them caused Frank to pull his feet off the dashboard and his quick movements resulted in a lost shoe and honking the horn. Not wanting to be seen, Frank threw himself across the seat. As he lay there, he cursed himself for being such a klutz.

When he thought the coast was clear, he slowly raised himself up onto one elbow to peek out the window. With a start, he cursed again and jumped up. There was no point in being careful, Jacob was staring at him and he looked angry.

"Leave her alone, Frank!" Jacob raised his fist and yelled through the window.

Frank grasped the door handle and opened the door, shoving it against Jacob's legs. "And who do you think you are? She was my girl first!"

"She was never yours." Jacob turned to walk away, but Frank caught him by his shoulder, swung him around and pushed him against the car.

"You can't keep us apart. I'll do whatever I have to do to make sure of that," Frank hissed. "Did you hear me? Whatever it takes, I'll do it. You are not going to be with her, I am."

* ◦ ◉ ● ◉ ◦ *

Rachel was once again sitting in Jacob's office, looking at the Spiderman décor while he was on the phone. This time however, it wasn't a parent he was talking to. It was the police.

"Look, I understand that the guy hasn't touched her and I understand that she doesn't have a protective stalking order. But what I am asking for is someone to file a report. This man threatened me and he assaulted me. He said he would do whatever it takes to get me out of the picture so he could be with Miss Riley. He hasn't stopped pushing himself on her and there's no telling what he plans to do next. I'll press charges. I want him to be held responsible for his actions!"

Rachel shivered a little as she remembered the way Frank had thrown Jacob up against the car. Jacob was a strong man, but he had been no match for Frank. She knew that Jacob would be sore tomorrow from the bruises he was sure to have.

"Is there any way you can get the court date for the protective stalking order hearing to be sooner? Is there any way to expedite this? She's not safe and she won't be until he knows there will be consequences for his actions."

Jacob looked frustrated while he listened to the voice on the other end of the receiver telling him there was nothing they could do. The court system was separate from the police force.

"Thanks for your time anyway," Jacob said politely, even though he wanted to yell at the man and tell him that he was of no help. After he hung up the phone, he looked at Rachel and said, "I don't care, I'm calling Shawn. What's his number?"

With a questioning look, Rachel told him the number. *There's nothing that Shawn can do, either. The only people who can change this are Frank and God. And I'm trusting God to keep me safe!*

"Officer Sinclair!" Jacob shouted when Shawn answered the call. "It's Jacob Grayson. Hey look, I know you asked Rachel to talk to someone else because of the whole conflict of interest thing, but I've just got to talk to you."

Jacob took a few minutes to relate to Shawn the events of the afternoon. Every now and then Rachel would hear Shawn's voice from where she was sitting. *Maybe this was a good idea after all; he seems to be just as upset as Jacob is.*

"So you think you might be able to work something out?" Jacob asked with a grin.

Rachel sat on the edge of her seat, wishing she could hear what Shawn was saying. But all she could make out was the tone of his voice, not the words.

"Thank you so much. I'll keep you posted." Jacob hung up the phone and looked at Rachel with satisfaction.

"So?"

"So he said he is going to go speak with Judge Gainsley. I guess they know each other on a personal level. He's going to push for him to grant you a protective stalking order."

Rachel clapped her hands and ran over to hug Jacob. "Thank you!"

"And he said he's going to watch your neighborhood and ask his police buddies to do the same. You'll be safer now."

Chapter 32

Rachel sat at the kitchen table with a cup of coffee cradled in her hands and her Bible lying open before her. It was early in the morning and since both her parents were still asleep, the house was quiet. It was times like this when she missed Shadow the most. The fuzzy Miniature Schnauzer used to sit in her lap when she studied. Closing her eyes, she remembered the way his fur felt when she would pet him.

Rachel let out a sigh and breathed a prayer of thanks for God's protection. Losing Shadow was painful, but things could have been much worse. *She* could have been the one on the receiving end of those fatal bullets.

While her mind played out the various possibilities, her Bible study was forgotten. The sound of the phone ringing broke into her thoughts and startled her, causing her to jump. Holding a hand over her racing heart, she got up and went to answer it. *That's what I get for dwelling on the evil that could happen.*

"Riley residence, this is Rachel speaking," she said with a forced cheerfulness.

"Hi, Rachel, it's Shawn. Look, I've got some great news! Judge Gainsley has agreed to do the hearing for your protective stalking order. And since he was judge for the trial, he's familiar with all the evidence and you won't have to testify again. He just wants to hear Jacob testify about the assault the other day." Rachel could hear the smile in his voice. "And what's even better, he told me he wasn't happy with the jury's decision for the trial."

Joy surged through Rachel's body and her sadness over Shadow lifted. "Shawn, that's great!"

"He can only do it tomorrow morning. So if it's at all possible, clear your calendar of any plans you had. And tell Jacob to do the same thing."

* ● ◉ ● ● ● ●

When Rachel walked into the courtroom the next day, she was filled with emotions she wasn't prepared for. The creak of the hardwood floor combined with the smell of furniture polish, and in an instant, her mind took her back to the day she had testified. Tears rushed to her eyes and her heart raced. Blinking, she willed herself not to cry as pain and panic surged through her and she wondered if she would make it through the hearing. Looking at the empty room, she saw Frank wasn't there yet and she knew the moment he walked through the door the situation would only get harder.

"Mom, I just don't think I can do this." Rachel reached out for Mary's hand.

"Yes, you can." Mary looked into her eyes and said, "You can do all things through Christ who strengthens you."

"Okay... you're right," she whispered in a shaky voice. "I just need a moment to focus; I need to draw on God's strength."

Rachel released her mom's hand and wiped her sweating hands on her pants. Taking a few deep breaths, she closed her eyes and thought of her favorite verse from the Psalms. *Those who look to him are radiant; their faces are never covered with shame.*

Peace settled over her and she could feel its warmth spread across her body. Her pulse slowed and her breathing evened out. She was ready; she could do what needed to be done. No matter what Frank did or said today, she would hold her head high. As long as she was in God's will, there was no reason to be ashamed or upset.

A noise at the back of the room caused Rachel to open her eyes. Gazing at the door, she saw Frank walk into the large courtroom. With a look of disgust that portrayed his feelings about being there, he seemed to slink into the place like a rat looking for food. As soon as he saw Rachel, he paused. Standing there, staring at her, his expression changed and his face lit up with a mischievous smile. Rachel wasn't sure what he was thinking, but with a sigh of relief, she realized it didn't really matter. The fear she had anticipated wasn't there. *Thank you, God! Thank you for your strength.*

Watching Frank walk over to the chair that was designated for him, Rachel became aware that she was still standing in the middle of the aisle. Her parents, who were standing next to her, were patiently waiting for her to move.

Turning to them, she quietly said, "I'm sorry. I'm ready now."

"Honey, there's nothing to apologize for," Dan whispered, keeping Frank from hearing their conversation. He placed a hand in the small of Rachel's back and ushered her to the seats where they were supposed to sit. "Shawn and Jacob should be here any minute."

As if she just now noticed they weren't present, Rachel looked at the door. "I hope they're not late," she worried out loud.

Minutes before the hearing was to start, Jacob came through the heavy oak doors. Without so much as glancing at Frank, he walked over and sat in the empty chair next to Rachel. He looked at her and smiled. He was leaning down to whisper something in her ear when Shawn appeared through the door at the front of the room and walked over to where the bailiff usually stands. When he took a place there, Rachel assumed he held that role today. She was so intent on watching Shawn, she almost missed seeing Judge Gainsley enter the room through the same door Shawn had used.

Once Judge Gainsley was seated in the judge's stand, he looked at Rachel. His face was unreadable, yet a kindness seemed to be lurking behind his professional demeanor.

Then, with an expression that was clearly full of annoyance, he looked at Frank.

"This is my courtroom," he said with authority. "I expect nothing less than complete respect for my wishes today. There will be no outbursts."

Frank lowered his head, and to Rachel, he looked like a child who was being reprimanded. Feeling hopeful that Frank wasn't feeling very confident, she smiled a little.

Judge Gainsley let his gaze include everyone in the room and said, "This is how we will proceed today. I am well aware of the testimonies of Mr. Smith and Miss Riley. I need no reminders. Therefore, I will not be asking for those testimonies. The only person to testify this morning will be Mr. Grayson."

Judge Gainsley tipped his head to his left, where Shawn was standing, and said, "According to Officer Sinclair, there was an incident recently. I feel it is of importance to this case, so I will hear Mr. Grayson's testimony. Then, if I feel there is a need, I will ask Mr. Smith to comment on the testimony. After that I will make my decision."

Judge Gainsley looked at Shawn and nodded his head. Shawn nodded in return, then stepped forward and addressed Jacob.

"Mr. Grayson, please stand." When Jacob stood, Shawn swore him in. Once that detail was taken care of, he said, "Please give Judge Gainsley a brief account of what happened."

Rachel watched with pride as Jacob began to testify. He spoke with clarity, and he gave a detailed description of what had happened. But that wasn't what made her proud. It was Jacob's attitude. Here stood a man who had every right to be angry and slanderous, but he wasn't. He told the truth with humility and grace. *The world would be a better place if there were more men like him.*

When Jacob was finished recounting the incident, Shawn asked him to be seated. Rachel dared to glance in Frank's direction and saw him fidgeting. His leg was bouncing up and down as if he had no control over it, and he appeared to be suffering from a severe case of itchiness. To Rachel, it was clear that Frank was guilty.

It must have been clear to the Judge as well, because there was barely a pause after Jacob finished speaking before Judge Gainsley looked at Frank. Biting off each word, he said, "Mr. Smith, I will ask you a question and I want a simple yes or no. Is that understood?"

Frank tried to still his leg and looked at the Judge as he said, "Yes."

Judge Gainsley picked up his gavel and held it in his right hand. And for a few minutes, he examined the wooden gavel. Then, as if finally deciding how to word his question, he looked at Frank and said, "Can you truthfully contest Mr. Grayson's testimony?"

Frank stared at his feet for a long time. It appeared he was trying to decide whether he should lie or not. With a sigh, he simply said, "No."

The word was forced out through clenched teeth and it was clear the admission was painful for him.

With a loud voice, Judge Gainsley said, "With the power invested in me, I grant Miss Riley a permanent protective stalking order, effective immediately." Turning to Frank, he said, "Mr. Smith, you will not be asked to move. However, you are not to be loitering in your front yard. You will not come within fifty feet of Miss Riley. Failure to comply with the regulations in the protective stalking order will result in a felony, a fine, and imprisonment."

With a smile and a nod in Rachel's direction, the Judge stood up and walked away.

* • ◦ ●◦ • *

Frank sat in his car and slammed his fists against the steering wheel. With a long string of curse words, Frank's anger toward Judge Gainsley spewed out of his mouth. The hearing had been a set up. He should have called his lawyer before agreeing to go. But who would have guessed that Shawn would have been able to arrange such a biased hearing?

"It's all Sinclair's fault. I swear I'll get even with him. One day, he'll regret getting involved." Feeling thirsty and longing for a beer, Frank started the car.

As he was driving toward the bar, he smiled and promised himself, "But first, I'm going to make Jacob curse the day he met Rachel."

Chapter 33

"Violet! I got the stalking order!" Rachel laughed into the phone. "I'm so happy I can't stop giggling!"

"That's great! Shawn told me all about it. He called a few minutes ago."

That figured. She should have thought about that. In spite of her joy about the stalking order, Rachel couldn't help but feel a tiny prickle of jealousy. *This was my news, not Shawn's.* Shaking her head to rid herself of such foolish thoughts, she reminded herself of what Jacob had said. Now that Violet had a boyfriend, Rachel wouldn't feel bad if she took time from their friendship to pursue a relationship of her own. *Frank isn't in the way anymore, and double dating could be the answer to spending time with Violet.*

"Violet, I have an idea. How about the four of us go out and celebrate tonight," Rachel said with excitement.

"The four of us? Does that mean what I think it means? Are you dating Jacob?"

Rachel cleared her throat, "Well, not yet. But we have spent a lot of time together. There have been moments when I thought he was going to ask me to be his girlfriend, but I wasn't ready so I would change the subject."

"Rachel! What do you mean you're not ready? You told me yourself a while back that I was right, that you think he's the guy you've been waiting for."

"I know. But life was so complicated with Frank and all that." Rachel looked up at the ceiling as if all of life's answers were written there. "Vi, I was worried that Frank would do something crazy… I just didn't want Jacob to get hurt."

Violet's voice lost its joking tone, and was now soft and understanding. "I understand. I'm sorry I teased you about it."

"There's nothing to be sorry about. But please say you'll come tonight?"

"I think it should work. Shawn's shift doesn't start until late tonight."

* • ◦ ●◉● ◦ • ·

Frank had never seen four people laugh so much. He'd also never seen a woman look at a man like Rachel was looking at Jacob. There was such tenderness in her eyes, and judging by the way she hung onto his every word, she loved him. What made it worse was the fact that Jacob obviously returned her feelings. And while they refrained from much physical contact, Frank was sure they were dating.

From up in the balcony of the old theater, Frank could easily watch the two couples as they waited for their sappy, romantic movie to start. In his opinion, the Fort Bragg Theater was too old and either needed to be remodeled, or torn down. But tonight, he decided that he liked the place. What other theater offered a balcony; and what better place to sit and watch someone than from a balcony? It was perfect.

When the movie started, Frank got up and walked out of the building. There was no point in staying. He'd seen enough tonight to know that something had to be done about Jacob. Even though he knew his chances with Rachel had reduced to almost nothing, just the thought of another man taking his place beside her filled him with jealousy.

What he needed was a new plan. And as he drove home, he started thinking about what he was going to do. The more he thought, the slower he drove. His mind turned over the many different ways the night could go, and with a devious smile, he pondered each option. Whatever he decided to do, Rachel couldn't be involved. With the stalking order in place, he was better off leaving her alone for the time being.

When he drove into Casper, it was only a little after 8:00 p.m. but the sun had set hours ago. The night air was heavy with humidity, and fog was moving in from the ocean. Right now, it rested along the rooftops of houses, but soon, it would cover the streets like a blanket.

He was so deep in thought, he almost missed his own driveway. But with a quick turn and a tap on the brakes, he pulled onto the breaking concrete slab in front of Phil's house and parked his car. As he got out, he looked at his truck. *I should sell one of these; I don't need both a car and a truck.*

As he walked up the steps to the front door, he saw a light on inside and wondered if Phil was home. Over the last couple of months, Phil had been gone a lot. Which was fine with him. Phil wasn't exactly easy to live with. He had too many rules. But he also had a house, and since Frank didn't have a job, he figured putting up with Phil was worth having a place to stay.

When Frank opened the door, it squeaked and the shrill noise brought Phil out of his bedroom. With anger written all over his face, he stormed down the hall.

"Are you insane?" Phil yelled. "Just this morning, you came home ranting and raving about the judge giving Rachel that stalking order. But does that stop you? No!"

Frank wasn't sure what was going on, but apparently Phil knew where he had been. "How do you know what I was doing?"

"Do you really think you're the only person who knows how to follow people?" Phil asked with a mix of sarcasm and impatience.

"So you followed me... big deal," Frank shrugged his shoulders.

"You are breaking the law."

Frank felt his anger start to grow. "I didn't bother her and she didn't even know I was there. What's it to you anyway?"

"What's it to me?" Phil took a step toward Frank. "What's it to me?"

In spite of the anger raging inside of Frank, seeing his brother so upset was almost humorous. Phil, the one who prided himself on staying aloof, was so angry he was shaking.

"I'll tell you what it is to me! It means I am housing a felon!" Phil raised his right hand in the air, his palm facing Frank as if signaling him to stop. "But no more, I packed all your things and they're in your truck. I'm tired of avoiding you. This is my house, I pay the bills and I abide by the law."

Frank's jaw hung open; he was finding it hard to believe Phil was kicking him out. "But...where do you expect me to go? What about my car?" Frank started listing off all the reasons why Phil couldn't make him leave.

"Frank, I don't care where you go. And you can come get the car later, or I can sell it for you." Phil sighed, "Just go."

Before Frank could say anything more, Phil walked down the hall. Grasping the door knob, Phil opened his bedroom door, entered the room and then slammed the door behind him. The conversation was over.

Swearing, Frank stormed out of the house and got into his truck. As he inserted his key into the ignition, defeat washed over him. It had been the worst day of his life. First, he'd received a piece of paper saying he couldn't be around the woman of his dreams. Then, he had spent the evening watching that same woman be wooed by another man. And to top it all off, he comes home to find out that he no longer has a place to sleep tonight.

He sat in his truck for almost an hour, slumped over the steering wheel with tears of frustration streaming down his face. No Rachel. No home. No hope.

Chapter 34

Rachel couldn't have imagined a better day. She had won the stalking order. After a whole year of asking Frank to leave her life, she was finally going to be free of him. And if that wasn't enough reason to feel like her day was the best, she'd spent the past four hours laughing and celebrating.

She felt sad as Jacob stopped his car in front of her house. *All good things must come to an end,* she thought as she unbuckled her seatbelt. Wanting to draw out the evening as long as she could, she delayed in opening her car door. But when she turned to look at Jacob, he was already halfway out the car. With a spring in his step, he walked over and opened her door. A great big smile made him even more handsome as he reached in and pulled her out. Rachel giggled as he drew her into his arms, tucking her into his leather jacket. He smelled of cologne and leather, and Rachel sighed as she snuggled against his chest. She had waited so long to find the man God wanted for her. And now that she was being held by him, she was so thankful she had waited. Jacob was the first man who had held her, and maybe soon he'd be the first one to kiss her.

"Rachel, I've been waiting a long time to tell you this." Jacob placed a kiss on top of her head. "I'm crazy about you."

Knowing this was a special moment, one to treasure, Rachel tried to stifle the laughter that bubbled up inside her. When she felt Jacob tense up, she knew she had to explain. "I'm sorry, but I couldn't help but think your choice of words was funny."

There was a brief moment of silence, and Rachel wondered if she'd ruined the most romantic moment of her life. Then all of a sudden, Jacob tightened his arms around her and let out a hearty laugh.

"Oh, but unlike Frank, I'm delightful when I'm crazy." Jacob released her enough to grasp her forearms and push her away so he could look into her eyes. "When I say I'm crazy for you, I'm saying I'll do whatever it takes to care for you and protect you." He slowly bent down and kissed her forehead, then whispered against her skin, "I'll do crazy things like thinking of you first and trying to make you happy." With another laugh, he said, "And depending on who you ask, some people just might think it's crazy to try my hardest to love you like Jesus loves His church."

Rachel cherished the feel of his lips on her face. With butterflies fluttering in her stomach, she turned to look him in the eye once again. The moment was so heavy with emotion, she almost couldn't speak. Swallowing, she forced the most important words of her life to pass her lips. "I love you, Jacob. And I think I'm going to love your craziness, too."

Before she had time to prepare, Jacob's lips were on hers. It was a tender kiss, full of love and promise. When Jacob broke the kiss, they stood mere inches apart, savoring the sweetness of newly declared love.

Suddenly, there was a loud bang from across the street and both Jacob and Rachel jumped as they were startled. No longer were they focused solely on each other, now they were acutely aware of the world around them—a world that included Frank. With a groan, Rachel turned to look at Frank's house. Anger filled her when she saw him standing beside his truck. How dare he intrude like this?

"He must have seen us kissing," Jacob whispered. "I could stand here all night and hold you in my arms. But I promised to protect you, and that's what I'm going to do."

Taking Rachel by the hand, he led her to her front door. With a smile and a look of tenderness in his eyes, he opened the door and waited for her to enter.

Rachel walked into the house and turned to look at him. "Goodnight, Jacob. Thank you for… everything. Tonight was perfect."

Leaning in, Jacob kissed her once again. "Goodnight, my love."

Rachel watched him walk to his car and then she closed the door. After securing the deadbolt, she went to the window to watch him drive away. As his taillights disappeared into the fog, she felt lonely. *Silly, you'll probably see him tomorrow,* she chided herself.

She had just turned to leave the window when the sound of a revving engine assaulted her ears. Curious, she turned back to the window and looked out to see Frank backing out of his driveway. *Frank's going after Jacob!*

Panic filled her and she ran to call Shawn. Picking up the phone, she started to dial the number, but she was shaking so much she almost dropped the phone. Forcing herself to calm down, she tried again. This time she was successful and she paced while the phone rang.

"Shawn!" she shouted when he answered. "Shawn, you have to do something! Frank is going after Jacob! He just dropped me off and Frank followed him."

"All right, calm down. I'm just now pulling into the police station to start my shift. As soon as I get my uniform on and get my gun, I'll go find them."

"Shawn, please hurry," Rachel was crying now. "I love him, don't let Frank hurt him."

* ◦ ◦●◦ ◦ ◦

Frank felt sick to his stomach. As he backed out of his driveway, all he could think about was seeing Jacob kissing her. Rage filled him as he thought of the injustice of it all. Ever since he'd first laid eyes on Rachel, he had wanted to know what it felt like to be loved by her. He wanted to know if her lips were as soft as they looked and if her body felt as good as he thought it would when it was pressed against his. Now, a year later, he had just watched another man experience what he'd been dreaming of and it filled him with anger.

Stomping on the brakes, he shifted his truck from reverse into drive and sped down the street. Gripping the steering wheel, he swore that Jacob would feel pain. Pain just as intense as the pain he was feeling right now. And even though he knew it wouldn't change things between him and Rachel, the thought of seeing Jacob suffer made him feel better. He may not be able to do something about the stalking order, but he could do something about Jacob.

And maybe, just maybe, if Jacob was out of the way, Rachel might change her mind. Maybe the only reason she didn't love him was because she had already been in love with Jacob. *Being her second choice isn't what I wanted, but I'll take it. It's better than nothing.*

◆ ◦ ◉ ● ◉ ◦ ◆

Jacob must have seen that Frank was following him, because he had led Frank all around Fort Bragg for the last half hour. And now, Jacob was getting back onto Highway 1. Apparently he was going back to Casper.

Frustration filled him. He didn't want to play this cat and mouse game any longer. It was time to get this thing going, it was time to make Jacob pay.

With a turn of the wheel and a firm foot on the gas pedal, Frank pulled his truck alongside Jacob's car. The road was void of other traffic, and the foggy, coastal night was dark. A small portion of the road was illuminated by their

271

headlights, and glimpses of the trees on the side of the highway could be seen from time to time. But all of this was lost on Frank. Even if there were other cars, he wouldn't have seen them. All he could see was the small, black car that Jacob was driving.

Calling Jacob names, Frank slammed his truck into the car. Sparks flew and tires squealed as Jacob fought to keep his car on the road. Frank laughed when he saw the scared look on Jacob's face. Knowing he had caused Jacob's fear gave him a feeling of power, and that feeling was intoxicating, even more intoxicating than beer.

Bracing himself, Frank once again slammed his truck into Jacob's car. But this time, he didn't give up. He just kept pushing. More sparks. More sounds of screeching tires.

"How do you like that?" Frank yelled as if Jacob could hear him.

Liking the feel of the game, Frank let off and watched as Jacob tried to get away. The little car zoomed ahead. And as Frank slowed his truck, he saw two large stripes on the road. The black lines were illuminated by the headlights and Frank realized that Jacob had burned his tires in his desire to leave Frank behind. Gauging by the amount of rubber that was left on the road, Jacob's tires were probably in bad shape.

Just as Frank was calculating what that information could mean, he saw Jacob's car swerve. Laughing out loud, Frank watched as the left rear tire blew. The whole tire had shredded and went flying all over the road, leaving the bare rim on the asphalt. The car lurched to the left as the absence of the tire caused the car to be off balance. In a rapid domino effect, Jacob went from speeding away from Frank, to crashing into a tree on the side of the highway.

Delight settled over Frank as he drove to Jacob's crashed car. After he parked, he jogged to the driver's side and looked in. There, with his head pillowed in the air bag, was a dazed Jacob. Not certain whether he was relieved or disappointed, Frank could see that Jacob had suffered no real harm.

Full of determination to follow through with his plans, he opened the car door and grasped Jacob's shirt. The movement of Frank pulling him out of the car caused Jacob to regain consciousness.

"You don't... " Jacob said as Frank swung him around and threw him up against the car. With a groan, Jacob's air was forced out of him and he couldn't finish his sentence.

"Shut up! I don't want to hear what you have to say!" Frank punched him.

Blood went flying as Jacob's lip split open. "You don't need to do this, Frank."

"You took her from me! She was my only hope for a better life!" Frank shouted as he brought his knee crashing into Jacob's stomach. "It hurts doesn't it? Well that's nothing compared to the pain I felt when I watched you kiss her tonight!"

Another punch caused blood to spatter on Frank's fist. Jacob was struggling to breathe past the pain.

"Rachel isn't... she isn't your only hope... Look to Jesus. He loves... "

Rage boiled up in Frank and he spit in Jacob's face. "I told you to shut up! Just shut up! Shut up!" Punch after punch, Frank let his anger explode.

When Jacob sagged, Frank let him fall unconscious to the ground. Cursing and screaming, Frank began to kick him. First in the groin, and then in the gut, followed by several blows to the head. With each kick, Frank's self-control receded.

Even though Jacob lay bleeding and defenseless, Frank would have continued to beat him up, but the sound of a siren caused him to stop. As if waking from a trance, Frank looked at his bloodied hands and then down at the man lying lifeless at his feet. *There's so much blood!*

With adrenaline pumping, Frank raced to his truck. Thankful he left his keys in the ignition, he started the engine, slammed the door shut and sped away.

When he glanced in his rearview mirror, he saw Officer Sinclair kneeling beside Jacob. Then, with a sinking feeling in his stomach, he saw another police car arrive at the scene. When the car rolled to a stop, Shawn flagged them on. Fear pricked the back of his neck and he knew that no matter what happened, he couldn't let them catch him.

Frank looked at the road ahead and calculated how much longer the straight stretch would last. Grabbing a box of belongings that Phil had packed in his truck, he placed it on the gas pedal. Knowing the fog would hide his next move; he quickly opened the door and jumped out. After a few rolls, he came to a stop on the side of the road and he ran into the bushes. With satisfaction, he watched as the lights of his truck disappeared into the fog.

Mere seconds later, the police car went speeding right by his hiding place. *I guess it's time for Frank Smith to disappear.*

Epilogue

It didn't take long for word to circulate among the churches about what had happened to Jacob. And when Rachel was asked to share at a special event that one of the local youth leaders had put together, she wasn't surprised. After such a traumatic experience, closure was needed and everyone was hopeful that the event would provide the youth with the emotional healing they needed.

It had only been two weeks, but to Rachel it seemed like it had been forever. The days blurred together and Rachel had to work really hard to remember all that had happened. Shawn had informed her that the police were unable to find Frank. When his truck had run off the bridge and crashed into the river, they were certain they would catch him. But he was nowhere to be found. After searching for ten days, the police force gave up. There was nothing to do but hope that someone would see him, recognize him and turn him in.

While Frank's unknown whereabouts should have been unnerving, Rachel felt a strange peace about it. She figured that if he was going to harm her, he would have done so already.

But what was bothering her the most was the guilt she felt. If she hadn't let Jacob get close to her, there would be no need for her to speak at the special service tonight. But she had been thinking only of herself. She had allowed that voice of caution to be silenced by her desire for him.

With a heart that felt torn apart, Rachel prepared her speech. Usually when she would speak at special gatherings, she would have a relaxed style of teaching that required very little notes. But tonight, a night that was bound to be filled with emotion, she knew she would need notes. In fact, every word she wanted to say would need to be written out. Even though she disliked it, she knew that tonight would be a time where she read from a page rather than speak from her heart.

Once the words were written, there was nothing left to do but comb her hair and change her clothes. She decided to skip dinner; there was no point in even trying to eat. Moving slowly, she stood up from the table that held her Bible and dictionary. After releasing a sigh, she went to her bedroom and looked at the clothes laid out on her bed.

A single tear rolled down her cheek as she realized it was the same outfit she had worn that night. It had been a perfect night filled with joy, whispered words of love, and sweet kisses—until Frank decided to ruin it. Then it turned into a night filled with pain, torment, and tears.

Jacob, I'm sorry! I'm so very sorry.

Standing up on the stage at the First Baptist of Fort Bragg, Rachel held her speech in a shaking hand. There must have been about a hundred youth gathered and looking from face to face, she recognized many of them.

Clearing her throat, she started to speak. "I'm sure that most of you know who I am, but I'm Rachel Riley and I work at Casper Community Church. Those of you who do know me may be familiar with my story." Looking at the pews where the youth from her church sat, she laughed, "I know my group could tell you my story, I've shared it with them just a few times."

Small bursts of laughter sprinkled the audience. Feeling less heavy hearted, Rachel continued speaking. She briefly told the youth about her choice to be different and to live the life that God had for her rather than choosing to conform to the world. It was a testimony she had shared many times but tonight, she also shared about Frank and the events of the past year.

Reaching down, Rachel picked up her dictionary from the pulpit. She took a few steps toward the right side of the platform. Holding the big book up for everyone to see, she said, "This is my favorite book, other than the Bible. In this book you can look up words and read their definition."

With a large smile she said, "Of course, you already knew that. But I would like to share something with you about this book and why it's one of my favorites. You see, words can mean many different things. To one person a certain word could be good and to another, it could be bad. Take the word 'crazy' for instance; the last time I talked with Jacob he said he was crazy for me." Rachel had to pause a while for all the whispers, cat calls, and giggles to stop. Shaking her head, she smiled and held up her hand, signaling for them to be quiet. "In light of the last year and dealing with Frank stalking me, I teased him for using that word. Frank was crazy for me, too… literally. And it wasn't a good thing. But Jacob quickly listed off the reasons why he chose the word. And they were all good things.

"So I stand here tonight, asking you, what words do you use to define yourself and what do they mean to you? A word I had labeled myself with was the word 'different.' And I hated it. I was different than everyone else and it bothered me… until I decided to embrace it." Looking at the teens sitting on the edge of their seat, Rachel knew they were listening. *Too bad Jacob can't see this.*

"Recently, I was shown how my definition of the word *different* wasn't the same as everyone else's.

"Frank Smith found me to be different than others, but that sounded good to him because he had been used and hurt by many. When he looked at me, he saw someone who he thought could make his life better. Unfortunately, he allowed his desire to make him crazy and things got out of control.

"Jacob, he too, found me to be different and that sounded good to him as well, because he also had chosen to be different. And just hours before he was attacked, he showed me how wrong I was about myself. My definition of different had caused me to sometimes wonder if I had gone down the right road in my life. But Jacob came alongside me and told me that he was traveling the same road."

A noise coming from the left side of the stage caught Rachel's attention. Stopping mid-thought, she turned and looked to see what it was. When her eyes opened wide in surprise, the crowd began to grow curious. Whispers could be heard as everyone tried to see what Rachel was looking at. But they didn't have to wonder for long.

In a loud booming voice, Jacob said, "And I thank God every day that we are traveling the same road."

Jacob, who was in obvious pain, worked his way to the pulpit. One leg was in a cast and he was using crutches. His face was bruised and had stitches in several places. "What Rachel has been saying is true. Things aren't always what they seem. She thought being different made her unwanted, but it actually made her more desirable. Frank was crazy in a bad way. And me," Jacob looked at Rachel and laughed, "I'm crazy in a good way."

Rachel walked over to Jacob and took his hand. Seeing Jacob out of the hospital helped her let go of the guilt she had been harboring these past two weeks.

"But there's someone else who knows that things aren't always as they seem. And that's God. You see, His Word says that He can take anything and make it good for those who are called by His name. What Frank did to me was evil and while I was experiencing it, I certainly didn't think there was any way it could be good. But God didn't see it that way. And while I have been lying in my hospital bed, I've been thinking. Frank and I were fighting over a woman who had the guts to stand up and be herself while the world around her demanded she conform."

Jacob awkwardly turned his body to look at Rachel. Gazing into her eyes he said, "I would get down on one knee, but that's not quite possible. But I think you understand."

Rachel's eye's filled with tears as she saw him reach into his pocket and pull out a small, dark blue box. When he opened it and showed her the diamond ring inside, the crowd gasped and whispers could be heard once again.

"Rachel, I almost missed my chance. But I'm not going to miss it now. I love you. Will you marry me?"

Rachel was in his arms before she answered. And as she said, "Yes, yes!" she happened to see someone standing at the side of the stage behind Jacob. Violet. Her friend smiled and did a little dance, expressing her happiness.

Pulling back from Jacob's embrace, she whispered, "Did you plan this?"

"With the help of Violet, Shawn, and a few others."

"You *are* crazy!" she said with a grin. Then, turning back to the crowd, she held up her left hand for everyone to see the ring Jacob had placed on her finger. As the cheers and clapping grew to an earsplitting level, Rachel closed her eyes and breathed a prayer. *Thank you, Lord. Thank you for keeping your promise. I am radiant and unashamed just like the Psalms say.*

The Author

When I was just six years old, The Finley Family began their full-time, faith-based ministry. For sixteen years, we traveled across the United States, performing concerts and sharing the love of Christ. During that time I played three instruments, sang, and wrote several songs.

In my early twenties I led a Bible study for young teen girls. As a result of this Bible study, I worked closely with girls in the foster care system. It was during this time that I was first introduced to the pain and suffering many teens experience at the hands of people who claim to care about them. Accounts of domestic violence, stalking, and all kinds of abuse were confided in me, and I spent time helping these girls break free from their past and press on to be more than what had been demonstrated for them by their abusers.

I met Luke Gertner when I was twenty-two. His charm and love for the Lord had not only caused him to be well-known in the Southern Baptist Association, it caused me to find him irresistible. After a brief long distance courtship, we married eleven months later.

In 2005, I completed training to counsel at the Crisis Pregnancy Resource Center in Porterville, California. Once again I was the confidant of many abused and hurting women as I counseled there for a brief period until we moved to a different city.

In 2006 we relocated to Sacramento, California. I worked alongside my husband as a youth leader, singing in the praise team and choir, as well as being on the leadership team for the preschool department of the church where Luke was on staff. One of the most rewarding parts of my participation at that church was teaching Sunday School for the youth. It was a blessed four years, and during that time I discovered my love for writing as I wrote my own teaching materials.

In December 2011, Luke was diagnosed with cancer and he fought a valiant fight, spending most of his time witnessing to the medical staff and brainstorming on how he could use his illness to bring glory to God. He succeeded to do both before he left this earth on May 28, 2013.

Now, as I begin a new season in life, I am focusing on my passion for writing and reaching others with the life lessons I have learned. I am currently writing for several magazines, and bringing new characters to life in the next two books in *The Strength To Stand* series. Check out www.TheStrengthToStand.com for more information on these books. You can also find some of my work on Facebook! Go to *I Choose Joy* and *like* my page to see the weekly posting of encouragement and lessons God is teaching me as I journey through life.

As a writer, my biggest desire is to share with others the importance of using our ability to choose, because life can present us with many options. Many of the options out there are demanding and attempting to deceive you because the world pressures you to "fit in." If we choose to follow the world, or simply do what feels easiest, we may fail to attain what God has designed for us as individuals.

And that's why I write. Each piece of work I present to my readers is designed to encourage people to take a step back and challenge the world's message. There is a purpose that only you can serve, and it's created by God just for you. In the end, it's all about the ability to choose. You can choose the world's plan for your life, or you can choose something more rewarding—God's plan.

Study Questions

Chapter 1

- What character trait does Mary Riley show?
- What traits are important to have?
- What do you think of Grandma Ruth's sharing family and personal information with Frank who, at the time, was a stranger?
- Where is the line between being overly trusting and too friendly versus cold and aloof?

Chapter 2

- Why do you think Rachel chose not to casually date?
- Is this a choice everyone should make?
- What, if any, are the benefits of dating?
- What, if any, are the benefits of choosing not to casually date?

Chapter 3

- Rachel chose not to share her concerns about Frank with her parents. In what way do you think this was harmful?
- Rachel gave Frank the impression she had someone special in her life. Share a time in your life when you used a fact to communicate a message that wasn't what that information necessarily meant.
- How do you define a lie?

Chapter 4

- If the Riley family had invited Frank and Phil to their house for Thanksgiving, how might that have changed the situation?
- What, if any, are some guidelines a person should follow concerning who we should invite into our homes?

Chapter 5

- As Rachel and Mary were walking to Frank's and Phil's house to deliver the cake, Mary told Rachel not to be so dramatic. How would you have felt if you were Rachel?
- When Frank claimed Rachel baked the cake just for him, what kind of personality traits does he portray?

Chapter 6

- How would you respond if one of your friends were kidnapped?
- Rachel and Violet kept the issue with Frank a secret. Why is secrecy such a pivotal element to Rachel's story?
- Discuss the reasons why always speaking truth is a healthy habit to have.

Chapter 7

- Due to the family's desire to help people, Dan and Mary felt validated in their disappointment in how Rachel treated Frank. How might they have responded to her actions more appropriately?
- A family gathering may have been more appropriate than having Rachel and Violet go someplace with Frank. What is the difference between the two options?

Chapter 8

- When Frank came to her house with flowers, what would have been the best way for Rachel or her parents to handle the situation?
- Discuss how Rachel interacted with Frank. What did she communicate to him?

- The Riley family was known for being concerned about others; however, it was not only Rachel's duty to reach out to Frank. Discuss a time in your life when you felt others should join you in something you felt was important.

Chapter 9

- All Rachel wanted to do was leave home for a few days and stop thinking about her problem with Frank. In what ways can running away change a situation?
- How would you respond if you received the letters from Frank?

Chapter 10

- How should Rachel have handled her anger towards her father?
- How should Phil have handled his anger towards Frank?
- Discuss a time in your life when you could have handled your anger better.

Chapter 11

- Since Frank's actions bother Rachel, what should she do when he tries to engage her in conversation?

- In what ways, if any, does repeatedly telling yourself not to worry change the situation?
- At this point, Rachel should have taken action of some kind. What do you feel would have been the best thing to do?

Chapter 12

- Since Rachel told Frank on the phone that she didn't want to talk to him, why do you think she allowed the conversation to continue?
- Why or why not do you agree with Violet's advice to Rachel?

Chapter 13

- Could Dan have done something differently when he confronted Frank?
- What do you think about Frank's reaction to the conversation he had with Dan?

Chapter 14

- When Frank came to the door, Mary got frustrated with his insistence that he wanted to talk to Rachel. That frustration led her to tell him where Rachel was. If you were Mary in this situation, what would you differently?

- Discuss a time you wished you could go back and change your response to someone.

Chapter 15

- Rachel's refusal to change her actions was born out of her desire to be a strong woman. Why, or why not, was that wise?
- In what ways should she have changed some things?
- How did you feel when Phil told Rachel about the lie?

Chapter 16

- When Rachel was too scared to think, Violet was practical and provided the guidance she needed. Why is it important to have a "Violet" in your life?
- In what ways are you a "Violet" for someone else?

Chapter 17

- Why, or why not, do you think Frank honestly didn't know why Dan was upset?
- What was your reaction when Frank confronted Rachel in the store?

Chapter 18

- What do you think would have been different about the situation if the Riley family had called the police sooner?
- Dan was the one who called; who do you think should have called?
- What are some reasons you feel led Rachel to hide her fear concerning her prayer?

Chapter 19

- How did you feel when Rachel admitted that she felt responsible for Frank's behavior?
- In what way, if any, do you think she is?
- If you or a loved one were in this situation, where could you find information to be adequately informed about how to handle problems like this?

Chapter 20

- If you have ever been to church camp, or something like it, in what ways did it have an impact on you?
- In what ways, if any, did Rachel's devotional at the camp speak to you?

Chapter 21

- When Frank was upset about the stalking charges, what could he have done instead of getting drunk?
- Many times, when we are troubled or hurting, we turn to something to make us feel better. What things are helpful and what things are harmful?

Chapter 22

- When Rachel accepted Jacob's offer for dinner, she had not told him about Frank yet. Why or why not was that knowledge important to Jacob?
- How did you feel when Shadow was killed?

Chapter 23

- Frank is drawn to Rachel because she is different. In what ways, if any, could this be a good thing?
- In what ways have you suffered through gossip or disapproval from your peers because you have taken a stand for your beliefs?
- If standing up for your beliefs important, then why is it so hard?

Chapter 24

- The woman Frank met at the bar was bullied into doing something she didn't want to do. In what ways have you been treated like this, or bullied?
- If you were Shawn, how would you respond to the woman?

Chapter 25

- If you were in this situation, would you run or stand up to Frank? Explain your answer.
- What do you think of Jacob's response when Rachel tells him about Frank?

Chapter 26

- When Rachel is upset about the five men on the jury panel, Mary reminds Rachel to trust God. Rachel, however, is still angry and doesn't feel any better by the comment. In what way is she being real, and what way is she simply being irrational?
- Jacob reassures Rachel that he doesn't care what is said about her; he knows the truth. Who are some people in your life who are that loyal?
- How loyal are you to the people in your life?

Chapter 27

- Shawn's testimony is dismissed due to a lack of discretion on his part when he was interacting with Frank. Discuss whether this was fair or not.
- Discuss a time in your life when you lost control of your temper and it caused problems for you later on.

Chapter 28

- As you read how the trial played out, how did you feel?
- Rachel feels her reputation is ruined. How important is a reputation?
- In what ways, if any, do you think her reputation really was ruined?

Chapter 29

- When Rachel told the jury what her prayer was about, what was your reaction?
- Discuss a time in your life when you have been moved to pray a desperate prayer for help.

Chapter 30

- When Rachel went to the store, in what ways did she let her anger control her actions?

- Discuss a time when you have forgotten to pray before acting.
- Discuss the results of those actions.

Chapter 31

- How did you feel when Jacob challenged Rachel concerning her prayer?
- Why or why not do you agree with what he said?
- What is real intercessory prayer like?

Chapter 32

- In this chapter, Rachel once again thinks of her favorite verse from the Psalms. What verse encourages you when you need strength?
- Discuss reasons why people feel ashamed.
- In what ways have you seen that those who look to the Lord are radiant and can be free from shame like Rachel's favorite verse says?

Chapter 33

- Frank makes a lot of plans. Why do you think his plans fail to work in his favor?
- Have you ever made plans that have failed? Why did they fail?
- At the end of this chapter, Frank has no hope. How can we find hope when all hope is gone?

Chapter 34

- When Jacob wraps Rachel in his arms, she feels thankful that she waited for God to bring Jacob into her life. What is something you have waited for?
- How did you feel when the wait was over?
- When Frank let his anger take control, everything took a turn for the worst. What are some things in life that we should never let take control?

Epilogue

- Rachel and Jacob reap the benefits of staying strong in their faith and they reached their goals. Even though it was hard, and dangerous, the end result brought joy and satisfaction. What are you working toward?
- Rachel's favorite book is the dictionary. If you were to look up the words *faithful* and *different*, why or why not would they describe you?
- In what ways do you stand out from the world and in what ways do you blend in?

Resources

Stalking

Stalking can happen to anyone, anywhere, and for any reason. If you feel you might be a victim of stalking, call your local police department immediately. The sooner the authorities are informed, the better. They can also give you important resource information that is available in your state and inform you about the stalking laws where you live.

If you think you might be a victim of stalking, these are some tips that may be helpful. Remember that a stalking situation is unpredictable and no one can begin to know what might happen next; nor can anyone say for certain what will or will not help the situation. However, these tips may prove to be useful. Whether you use these tips or not, please contact local women's advocacy groups or domestic relationship centers as well as your local police

department. Then consider following these tips, or similar information.

What you should *not* do:

- **Do not** ignore feelings of danger or odd actions. If someone makes you feel uncomfortable, pay attention to that.
- **Do not** follow advice that you feel will place you in harm. No matter how great the information or advice may be, only do what you feel is the safest.
- **Do not** keep the situation a secret. Tell a trusted friend, your pastor, the police, etc.
- **Do not** throw away letters, notes, or written proof of unwanted contact.
- **Do not** erase unwanted text messages, voicemail messages, or emails.
- **Do not** let your stalker bait you into a conversation. Once you have decided you don't want them to contact you, simply tell them to leave you alone or you will call the police. After that, refuse to engage in conversation with them and follow up on calling the police if they don't leave you alone.

What you *should* do:

- **Do** keep a record of how you have been contacted, what was said, and what was done. Keep a record of the date of each contact. The more information you can give the police the better.

- **Do** involve others. You need help and you also need witnesses to speak on your behalf.
- **Do** get informed. There are a lot of resources to help victims of stalking. Contact your local police department for information or search the internet or phone book for local organizations that offer help.
- **Do** what it takes to make contact less likely. If that means you have to get a different phone number, do it. Simple changes on your part can make a huge difference and those actions do not mean your stalker has control over you. Those preventative actions actually mean you are taking control of the situation.
- **Do** seek spiritual support. Meeting regularly with a pastor or counselor may keep you from feeling confused. They can help you remember that the reasons for stalking come from within the heart of the stalker, not because of something you have said or done.

Domestic Violence

Domestic and relationship violence and abuse can happen to anyone, anywhere, and for any reason. It is a sad epidemic that affects the lives of too many people. There are many forms of abuse, not only physical: emotional, verbal, spiritual, sexual, and physical. If you feel you might be a victim of domestic violence or abuse, call your local police department immediately. The sooner the authorities are informed, the better. They can also give you important resource information that is available in your state and inform you about the protective laws where you live.

If you think you might be a victim of domestic and relationship violence and abuse, these are some tips that may be helpful. Remember that a violence and abuse situation is unpredictable and no one can begin to know what might happen next; nor can anyone say for certain what will or will not help the situation. However, these tips may prove to be useful. Whether you use these tips or not, please contact local women's advocacy groups or domestic relationship centers as well as your local police department. Then consider following these tips, or similar information.

What you should *not* do:
- **Do not** ignore harmful actions. If someone harms you, it is not okay.
- **Do not** keep the situation a secret. Tell a trusted friend, your pastor, the police, etc.
- **Do not** follow advice that you feel will place you in harm. No matter how great the information or advice may be, only do what you feel is the safest.
- **Do not** make excuses for your abuser's irrational behavior.
- **Do not** let them bully you into hiding. Domestic and relational abuse never resolves itself. Simply

waiting for your abuser to change will result in more harm to you.

- **Do not** let them blame you. There is no excuse for their behavior.

What you *should* do:

- **Do** keep a record of how you have been harmed, what was said, and what was done. Keep a record of the dates each incident occurred. The more information you can give the police, the better.
- **Do** involve others. You need help and you also need witnesses to speak on your behalf.
- **Do** get informed. There are a lot of resources to help victims of domestic and relational abuse. Contact your local police department for information or search the internet or phone book for local organizations that offer help.
- **Do** what it takes to make the abuse less likely. If that means you have to move away and get a restraining order, do it. Be prepared to enforce the restraining order.
- **Do** seek spiritual support. Meeting regularly with a pastor or counselor can keep you from feeling confused. They can help you remember that the reasons for abuse come from within the heart of the abuser, not because of something you have said or done.
- **Do** prepare for a safe exit if it becomes necessary:

- If you have your own vehicle, give a copy of car keys, house keys, work keys, to a trusted friend who can keep their possession of the keys confidential. Make sure to keep your gas tank full.
- Pack a bag with a few full changes of clothing, extra grooming needs, medications, an extra cell phone charger, and whatever else you feel you may need. Give that bag to your trusted friend along with the keys.
- Keep a small amount of cash on hand.
- Keep your cell phone charged and with you if you have one.

Disclaimer:

These resources are presented for you to read, assimilate, and pursue only if you believe they are important to you. You bear full responsibility for your assessment and application, if any, of any of these resources. These resources are actions or recommendations of actions the author believes may be helpful, and strictly represent her own opinions. These resources may or may not represent the opinions of anyone involved in the production of this book. In no way do these resources represent any legal opinion or legal counsel whatsoever. Do not use these resources apart from seeking professional assistance from police authorities, professional counselors, licensed medical servicing personnel, or legal counsel. Author and all parties engaged in the production of this book bear no responsibility whatsoever for any outcomes of your situation whether these resources are or were used or not. If you feel you are the victim of stalking or domestic violence, contact your local police or other professional personnel, including local women's advocacy groups or domestic relationship centers.

Products and Services

Coming soon...

A Different Life Lived

Book Two
The Strength To Stand Series

What happens when keeping a secret is harmful to one person's life, but revealing the secret could bring the end to someone else's?

When Violet Thompson decides to return to Mexico, she thinks it will be a good thing. But when it costs her a relationship she thought she wanted, she begins to wonder. Then, when the missions trip involves something she didn't expect, she finds herself faced with the decision to pack up and go home, or to face her fears and press on.

Will Violet be able to keep her secret? Or will she have to risk the life of someone else in order to save her own?

Coming soon…

A Different Child Born

Book Three
The Strength To Stand Series

When faced with danger, how do you decide which action is the lesser of two evils?

For Mercy Taylor, it seems as if every choice she makes will end in sorrow. With a tragic childhood and a marriage that ended too soon, it comes as no surprise that she finds herself fighting for her life. But the traumatic events of her life include more than just herself this time, they include her child as well.

As she is literally running from her past, she's forced to make decisions she's not prepared to make. But in order to make the right choice, she must come to terms with her past and find a source of hope for the future.

*****

I Choose Joy

I Choose Joy is a Facebook blog about one woman's journey through life and her desire to remain joyful and radiant regardless of her circumstances.

Join the Facebook crowd today by going to *I Choose Joy* by Rebecca Gertner and click "like" to see all the encouraging devotional and life-lesson posts!

If you don't use Facebook, you can still be part of the *I Choose Joy* following. Simply send an email to info@rebeccagertner.com and ask to be added to the email list and have the postings sent directly to your email inbox!

*****

Speaking Engagements

Rebecca Gertner is available to speak at your next conference or event! For more information, please send an email to **info@rebeccagertner.com**.

CPSIA information can be obtained at www.ICGtesting.com
Printed in the USA
BVOW08s1311221013

334324BV00002B/2/P